SO-BAU-433

AMERICAN ADVENTURES

Thomas
in Danger

AMERICAN ADVENTURES

Thomas
in Danger

BONNIE PRYOR

ILLUSTRATED BY
BERT DODSON

Morrow Junior Books

NEW YORK

Published by Morrow Junior Books
a division of William Morrow and Company, Inc.
1350 Avenue of the Americas, New York, NY 10019
www.williammorrow.com

Printed in the United States of America.

10 9 8 7 6 5 4 3 2 1

Library of Congress Cataloging-in-Publication Data
Pryor, Bonnie.
Thomas in danger / Bonnie Pryor; illustrated by Bert Dodson.
p. cm.—(American adventures)
Sequel to: Thomas.
Summary: Having lost their home when the Revolutionary War reached
their part of rural Pennsylvania, Thomas and his family start a new life
running an inn in Philadelphia, where Thomas finds new danger
that takes him into captivity among the Iroquois.
ISBN 0-688-16518-4
1. Pennsylvania—History—Revolution, 1775–1783 Juvenile fiction.
[1. Pennsylvania—History—Revolution, 1775–1783 Fiction.
2. United States—History—Revolution, 1775–1783 Fiction.
3. Indian captivities Fiction.   4. Iroquois Indians Fiction.
5. Indians of North America Fiction.]   I. Dodson, Bert,
ill.   II. Title.   III. Series: Pryor, Bonnie. American adventures.
PZ7.P94965Ti 1999   [Fic]—dc21   99-15286   CIP

Contents

ONE

---◆---

Danger along the Road

From his perch in the wagon, Thomas Bowden stared anxiously into the woods on both sides of the road. There were too many places where an Indian or a Tory soldier could hide, for his liking. They had been traveling all day. The road was little better than a weedy path as it wound through the Pennsylvania countryside toward the city of Philadelphia. It was so deeply rutted and pitted with holes that the wagon bounced and rocked until every bone in Thomas's body ached in protest.

1
☆

His mother sat next to Mr. Peters, holding his baby brother, Ben. The rest of the wagon, except for the small space boarded off for Thomas and his sister, Emma, was piled high with smelly cabbages. When the wagon bounced over especially hard bumps, a few of the cabbages would fly off the back.

Mr. Peters would not stop to pick the cabbages up. Thomas knew he, too, was worried about a sudden attack. He drove the horses at a steady pace. Every now and then, he reached down and patted the musket on the seat beside him as though to reassure himself it was still there if he needed it.

"I wish we had something to read," Emma said. Thomas thought of all the wonderful books that had been destroyed when Mr. Hailey's house was burned down by the Tories. Mr. Hailey had been a good neighbor. Thomas sighed. With all this bouncing, it would be impossible to read anyway.

Thomas grabbed for a cabbage as it flew off the pile and missed. He watched it roll down the road. "It looks like we're leaving a trail of cabbages," he said wearily.

Emma almost smiled. "Wouldn't it be nice if Father was following the trail and found us?" she said.

Thomas nodded at his younger sister. Six months before, Mr. Bowden had joined the Continental army to fight the British with General George Washington. Their mother was left to manage the family homestead in frontier Pennsylvania. Thomas and Emma knew that for months the army had been camped outside Philadelphia while the British redcoats occupied the town. Mr. Bowden had thought that his family would be safe so far from the British soldiers. Then the Tories, who sided with the British, had joined with the powerful Iroquois Nation to attack scores of small frontier settlements.

"It isn't fair," Emma said crossly. "Here we are heading to Philadelphia, and Father is not there anymore."

"I wish we knew where Father is," Thomas said. "Sam Tucker said our soldiers were chasing the British all the way to New York. He said there was some fighting in New Jersey."

In spite of the worry over their father, Thomas smiled at the thought of Sam Tucker. He and his wife had helped the Bowdens when they needed it most. Sam often pretended to be a harmless old woodsman. It was safer to travel that way when he carried messages to General Washington.

"How much longer do you think it will be before Father can return home?" Emma asked.

Thomas shrugged. "As soon as the redcoats go back to England and let us have our freedom." He wished he felt as confident as he sounded. He tried to imagine his father's sorrow when he discovered that they no longer had a home.

Just a few weeks before, their home had been a cabin in the beautiful Wyoming Valley along the Susquehanna River. Now it was gone, burned in the massacre that had killed many of their neighbors.

Thomas knew that the patriots had not always been kind to the Tories. Still, it was difficult to understand how the Tories could have murdered their fellow countrymen. After the fighting that had driven the Bowdens out of their home, the Tory army had stood by while the few surviving soldiers were tortured by the Iroquois. The Bowdens had escaped with their lives only by crossing a swamp and walking over the thickly forested Pocono Mountains. Except for a few coins their mother had sewed in her dress and Ben's blanket, they had lost everything.

Walking across the mountains, Thomas had thought only of survival and easing his terrible hunger. When they had finally arrived at the little settlement called Stroudsburg, the fear had given way to anger. Before the massacre, the world had been a good place, an interesting place. His mother had often teased him about his curiosity. Now all he could feel was hate. He agreed with the men who wanted to kill every Indian and Tory.

He knew his mother was concerned about him. He saw her worried looks when she thought he didn't see. For her sake, he tried to hide his feelings, but his anger made him feel like his heart had turned to stone.

It was Sam Tucker who had helped them get to Stroudsburg. The people there had been kind. They had fed and cared for the Bowdens and the other survivors who had crossed the mountains. Some people had stayed, hoping to return to whatever was left of their homes. Mrs. Bowden, however, was determined to go to Philadelphia and live with her sister Rachel until Mr. Bowden found them. She had hired Mr. Peters and his wagon in Stroudsburg. He hadn't bothered to tell her that he was also bringing a load of cabbages to sell in the city.

"Ouch!" Emma yelled. The wagon had hit such a deep rut that she and Thomas were bounced up in the air and down again with a bone-rattling bump. Emma rubbed her hip ruefully. "Maybe walking to Philadelphia would have been easier."

Old Nobbin, their big black dog, who had faithfully followed them across the mountains, looked up as if to say he agreed with Emma, but Thomas shook his head. "I've had enough walking." Peering ahead, he saw two stone pillars and a gate across the crude road. Mr. Peters pulled on the reins and the wagon came to a halt. Mrs. Bowden had paid Mr. Peters twenty dollars for the trip, and he still demanded that she pay all the tolls. This was the third one that day.

Thomas leaned forward. "Couldn't we just drive around?"

"That would make me feel very unfriendly," said a voice. A burly man in a dirty shirt and buckskin leggings stepped out in front of the wagon. He cradled a musket in his arms.

"This is a public road," Mrs. Bowden said. She shifted Ben to her other arm while she dug a few more coins out of her purse.

"It crosses my land," the man answered. "It's my legal right to collect a fee." He scowled at them suspiciously. "Where are you headed?"

"Not that it's your concern," Mr. Peters replied. "I am taking this good lady and her children to Philadelphia to stay with her sister. They just escaped the massacre in the Wyoming Valley."

The man lowered his gun and nodded at Mrs. Bowden. "I know about that. My sister and her husband didn't wait to be attacked. They left their home and moved to Easton. They lost everything."

Easton was a small settlement not far from Stroudsburg. "We just passed through there," Mrs. Bowden told the man. "We saw many survivors.

I'm glad your sister is safe. Many did not make it across the mountains. Some say more than a hundred are lost."

"They ought to send an army up north and kill every one of those heathens," the man said bitterly.

Thomas nodded to show the man he agreed. Mrs. Bowden held out a coin to the man, but he waved them on. "You've had enough problems," he said.

"You are kind," Mrs. Bowden said gratefully.

The man removed the wooden crossbars from the gate, and the wagon creaked slowly forward. "Be careful," he warned. "There have been reports of Tory soldiers in the area."

Mrs. Bowden picked a branch from a leafy bush as they passed and used it to brush away the black-flies before they could bite little Ben. After a time, she twisted in the seat to look back at Thomas and Emma. "Are you all right?" she asked.

"I'm awful tired, Mama," Emma answered.

"We need to stop for a few minutes to rest," Mrs. Bowden said to Mr. Peters.

The driver looked around nervously. They were

following a river, and the land was gently rolling hills and open meadows. Only a few stands of trees could hide any danger. He shrugged and pulled on the reins. "Looks safe enough. We'll stop here for a spell. Give the horses a rest. You can stretch a bit," he said gruffly.

Gratefully, Thomas jumped down. "May we walk around?" he asked.

Mr. Peters shrugged. "I don't aim to stay here more than a few minutes."

"Don't go far," warned Mrs. Bowden.

Nobbin jumped off the wagon and shook himself. While Mr. Peters tended the horses and their mother changed the baby's diaper, Thomas and Emma ran about with Nobbin. Thomas threw a stick and Nobbin caught it and brought it back.

Suddenly, Nobbin's ears stood straight up, a sign that he'd spotted a rabbit or a deer to chase. "Grab him," Thomas shouted to Emma, who was closer. "If he runs away, he might not be back for hours."

Emma made a dive for him, but she was too late. With a joyful yip, Nobbin was off, running through the lightly forested meadow. Thomas saw a gray flash of fur bounding through the grass ahead of the dog.

"Why didn't you catch him?" Thomas shouted.

Emma's face crumpled. "I tried."

Thomas kicked at a lump of dirt. "Stupid girl," he muttered, knowing he was being mean.

"Why are you always so hateful now?" Emma said. "You didn't catch him, either."

Thomas sighed. "I'm sorry. We should have tied a rope around him."

"What should we do?" Emma asked. She looked back at her mother and Mr. Peters. Neither of the adults had noticed what had happened.

Thomas didn't answer. He walked a short ways after the dog. The trail was plain to see because of the smashed and broken grass. The land sloped down a hill, and in a minute he could no longer see the wagon.

"We'd better go back," Emma said nervously. "Nobbin will find us. He always does."

Thomas pointed. Nobbin was only a few yards away, sniffing at a hole in the tall grass.

"Come on, Nobbin," Emma coaxed.

Miraculously, Nobbin seemed to forget the rabbit. He bounded back toward them.

"Good dog," Thomas said.

Holding on to Nobbin, they climbed back up the hill. Suddenly, Nobbin's ears perked up again and Thomas heard the sound of horses and a jaunty tinkle of metal. He put his finger to his lips and motioned for Emma to get down. Without a word, she pulled Nobbin behind a fallen tree and put her hand over the dog's muzzle. Thomas inched down beside her and peeked over the rotted log.

Less than five hundred feet away, a patrol of Tory Rangers in their green jackets rode single file. They were heading straight for the wagon.

Thomas looked frantically for some way to warn his mother and Mr. Peters. At the top of the hill, the captain called a halt. He sat in the saddle, staring down at the wagon. From where they were hidden, Thomas could see his mother walking along the riverbank with the baby, unaware of the danger. Mr. Peters was busy watering the horses.

A second officer reined in beside the captain. They were so close that Thomas could see the

sweat on the horses and smell the soldier scent of gunpowder and leather.

"Those cabbages will feed the men for quite a few days, sir," the officer said quietly.

"Our orders are to not draw attention to ourselves," the captain replied. "We can buy food from our friends in the area. At any rate, it could be a trap. I, for one, don't want to go down in history as dying for a load of cabbages."

The second officer wheeled his horse and rode back down to the waiting men.

Nobbin wiggled in Emma's arms as she struggled to hold him down. The captain turned his horse more slowly. On the other side of the log, he stopped, and for one breathless moment Thomas was sure he was looking straight at them. Thomas sucked in a breath, but the captain rode past their hiding place and resumed his place at the front of the line.

Thomas and Emma stayed without moving until the last soldier had disappeared from sight. Then they raced down the hill to the waiting wagon.

TWO

Philadelphia at Last

"I see it, I see it," Emma shouted excitedly. After the close call with the Tories, they had ridden in worried silence. Now, even sour old Mr. Peters turned to smile at her exuberance.

"That's the steeple of Christ Church, little missy," he said. "It's the city's best-known site. If you look closely, you will see there is no bell. The patriots were afraid the British would melt it down for bullets, so they hid it. Hid the Liberty Bell, too." Mr. Peters slapped his knee as though enjoying a good joke. "Now that the British are gone, they are going to bring them back."

Thomas gasped with amazement. He had been here when he was small, but he had not remembered how big everything was. Graceful two- and three-story mansions with beautiful landscaped grounds dotted the farthest reaches of the city. As they passed the wharves along the Delaware River, Thomas saw several tall-masted ships being loaded by men carrying bundles and barrels from wagons or nearby warehouses.

The horses' hooves sounded with a merry *clop-clop* on the paved city streets. They passed a small group of Continental soldiers marching smartly in their snappy blue uniforms. Off the main thoroughfares, shoppers hustled up narrow alleys crowded with houses and shops.

"There's Butterfly Alley," said Mrs. Bowden. She pointed to a narrow brick street lined with two- and three-story houses.

"It's much too narrow for my wagon. I will let you off here," said Mr. Peters. "It's time I was heading for the market."

Thomas tied a rope around Nobbin's neck and jumped out of the wagon. The old black dog strained at the leash, busily sniffing everything in sight. The houses on the alley were built quite close together, and only a narrow sidewalk separated them from the street. Many had shops at the street level, with large colorful signs to announce their business. RED BULL INN read one with a huge picture of a charging bull. J. SMITH, SADDLE MAKER announced another. Still another proclaimed that a silversmith resided there.

"Don't walk too close to the houses," Mr. Peters warned as he started to drive away.

"Why not?" Thomas questioned. The answer came before Mr. Peters could reply. A second-story window opened and a maid tossed out the contents of a chamber pot without even a glance to see who was walking below. It splashed on the street a few feet away.

"Phew," Emma said, wrinkling her face in distaste. It was obviously not the only time garbage had been emptied along the streets. There were mounds of it along the edge of the road. It was so high in places that the shop proprietors had placed wide boards across to allow people to get into their shops.

"In some places in the city, they have hired a scavenger to clean the streets," Mr. Peters said. "Looks like they could use one here." He slapped the reins on the horses' backs and was off.

"I think they should have named this alley Fly instead of Butterfly," Thomas said, and indeed it was true. It was a warm day and hordes of flies rose from the piles of garbage as they walked. A wave of homesickness washed over Thomas when he thought of the clean-smelling air of the valley.

Farther down the alley, the houses became more prosperous looking and the street was cleaner. Mrs. Bowden stopped in front of a handsome brick house and softly knocked on the door. It was answered immediately by a man they did not recognize.

"Oh," said Mrs. Bowden. "I am sorry to disturb you. I thought this was the home of Rachel Knowles, my sister." She looked around in confusion. "Have I come to the wrong house?"

The man stared at her. "My name is Jessup, and this is my house. Rachel Knowles and her husband were Tories. They fled in fear for their lives when the British left the city some months back. People don't take kindly to Tories these days. They sold me the house before they left."

Mrs. Bowden sagged weakly against the door frame. "Where did they go then?" she asked.

Mr. Jessup shrugged. "Some went to England. I heard many others went north. Quebec, possibly. I say good riddance."

Mrs. Bowden's eyes blazed. "I say you probably bought the house at robbers' prices. How fortunate that you are a patriot."

Now it was Mr. Jessup's turn to look angry. "I've done nothing wrong. While the Tories partied and entertained the British soldiers, George Washington's army camped outside of town, hungry and nearly freezing. My son was with them."

"So was our father," Thomas blurted out.

"Is that true?" Mr. Jessup asked. "You are patriots?"

When Mrs. Bowden nodded, the man's manner underwent a change. "Were you planning to stay with your sister, then? Have you another place to go?"

Mrs. Bowden shook her head. "I don't know anyone else in the city."

Mr. Jessup opened the door wide enough to let them enter. "Maybe we can help you. Come and talk with my wife."

Thomas tied Nobbin to a post and followed his mother and Emma inside. Mr. Jessup led them to the parlor and then went to fetch his wife. Thomas and Emma looked around the room. Although the furnishings were different, Thomas thought he remembered the house, even though he had been very young when he last visited. There were four large rooms downstairs and four up. On the top floor was the servants' quarters. The kitchen, he remembered, was in a small building in back of the main house.

A servant was in the corner, scrubbing the parlor floorboards with a brush she dipped in a bucket of water and strong-smelling soap. She looked up and smiled. Curly gray hair poked out of the white cap she was wearing.

"Lottie!" A small woman with a pinched, proud

manner swept into the room. "You should be done with that," she said sharply. She kicked the servant with the pointed toe of her shoe. "Go and fetch us some coffee."

It wasn't a hard kick. Nevertheless, Thomas was disturbed. He gave the woman a sympathetic look as she picked up her bucket and hurried out of the room.

"I'm Ann Jessup," the woman said, casting a haughty look at Mrs. Bowden's ragged dress. "I do hope when this is all over that we can enjoy a cup of tea again," she said. "Coffee is a poor substitute in my mind."

"I rather like it," answered Thomas's mother. She handed Ben to Thomas and tried to smooth the wrinkles out of her dress. Mrs. Jessup was quite elegantly attired, and the Bowdens looked shabby by comparison.

Thomas stood behind his mother. This war is strange, he thought. His aunt Rachel was a Tory, and he supposed he should hate her. But he remembered her as a sweet and gentle lady who was always kind to everyone. Mrs. Jessup was a patriot, and he didn't like her a bit.

"My husband tells me you lost everything," Mrs. Jessup said. "Have you thought about what you will do?"

Lottie came back holding a tray with a silver coffeepot and cups. She set it on the elegant marble-topped table next to Mrs. Jessup.

"Take the children to the kitchen and give them some hot chocolate," instructed Mrs. Jessup.

Thomas, who was still carrying Ben, and Emma followed Lottie outdoors and to the kitchen. Inside was a huge iron woodstove. Copper pots and pans hung from the rafters, and in the center of the room was a table used for chopping vegetables and meats.

"You sit yourselves right down," Lottie said kindly. Her hands were red from years of scrubbing. Her thin face was creased, but her blue eyes were young and the skin around them was crinkled with laugh lines. She set out a plate of biscuits and a pot of butter and another of blackberry jelly and bustled about the stove, making the hot chocolate. Under her gentle prodding, Thomas and Emma told her about their misfortunes.

"What is your poor mother going to do?" Lottie asked.

"I don't know," Thomas answered. "We thought we would stay with my aunt and uncle."

"I worked for your aunt. She was a nice lady. Your kinfolks were no more than gone when the Jessups moved here," Lottie said. She leaned forward. "Don't you go saying I told you this. Your aunt and uncle owned several shops in town and they were all sold. But they had just bought a tavern over on Race Street. Wasn't time to sell it, so it's just boarded up. It was called the Peach Tree Inn. The Jessups aren't likely to tell your mother, because they are hoping to get it when the taxes come due. I know Miss Rachel would want your mother to have it. If she could manage to get it going, I think there are rooms upstairs for you to live."

Emma started to get up. "I'll go tell Mama," she said happily.

Lottie looked alarmed. "Don't you say anything until you get away from here. I'll lose my job for sure." She leaned close and smiled. "You tell your mama that if she needs some help, I would be pleased to come and work for her." She reached up on a shelf and handed Thomas a large brass key. "Mrs. Jessup doesn't know that key is here. She never comes to the kitchen."

"Thank you," Thomas said.

Mrs. Bowden was getting ready to leave when they returned to the main house. Her lips were pressed tightly, and Thomas could see that she was fighting back tears. Mrs. Jessup sounded irritated. "I've made you a good offer. It is the only sensible solution."

When Mrs. Bowden shook her head and did not answer, Mrs. Jessup gave her a haughty look. "Very well, then. Don't come back here begging."

"I will not be back," Mrs. Bowden said stiffly. Mrs. Jessup slammed the door behind them as Mrs. Bowden marched proudly away. Thomas and Emma untied Nobbin and ran to catch up.

Once out of sight of the house, Mrs. Bowden halted and her proud look crumbled. "What a horrid woman," she said with a sob. "She offered me a job as her housekeeper. She said I could keep Ben with me but that I would have to send you two to the poorhouse."

Emma jumped up and down, gleeful that they had good news. Thomas gave their mother the key and quickly repeated what Lottie had told them. Mrs. Bowden wiped her eyes and straightened her shoulders. She took the key and slipped it into her apron pocket. "What are we waiting for?" she asked with a forced cheerfulness. "Let's go see our new home."

THREE

The Peach Tree Inn

Race Street was a rough area of town near the waterfront. Sailors staggered out of run-down buildings and noisy taverns. They stared as the little family passed by. Nobbin padded beside them, growling at the strange sights and smells. Thomas held the rope tightly in his hands for fear that the dog would be crushed by one of the heavy wagons rumbling toward the docks.

"I don't like it here," Emma said quietly.

The hopeful look Thomas had seen on his

mother's face when he had handed her the key slowly disappeared. It was replaced by a tight, worried frown. There were many taverns and inns near the waterfront, but none of them was empty and none was called The Peach Tree Inn.

After a few blocks, the buildings were in better repair and the neighborhood did not seem quite so rough. Mrs. Bowden began to look hopeful again.

"There it is," Thomas said. He pointed to a narrow brick building. The sign was hanging down on one side and in dire need of painting, but the words were still legible. Rough boards had been nailed across the small windows in front and the door sagged. Still, the building seemed sturdy and the roof was good. There was a small empty lot next door with a maple tree that shaded the front porch.

"Well," Mrs. Bowden said. "I had hoped for better, but it could be worse. Let's look inside."

They walked to the back of the inn and discovered a brick wall with a wooden gate. Emma clapped her hands in delight. The wall concealed a small neglected garden. Roses bloomed along the fence and a peach tree laden with fruit grew in the corner.

"The Peach Tree Inn!" Thomas exclaimed.

There was a small porch overlooking the garden. Mrs. Bowden nodded. "At least there will be a place for Ben to take in the sun." The back door was not boarded up. She used the key to open the door.

It was dark inside the inn. A thick coat of grease and dirt covered the windows. There was a large kitchen, with a woodstove like the one Thomas had seen at the Jessups'. Large black bugs crawled over the dirty pots and pans piled on the table. The serving room was cleaner, although covered with dust and grime. There was a small staircase in one corner.

"Oh, Mama, it's awful," said Emma as a bug skittered over her foot.

"Dirt can be washed away," Mrs. Bowden answered. "The tables are strong and the walls sound. That's what is important."

Thomas looked at the rooms in dismay. "Are you serious about running an inn?" he asked.

Mrs. Bowden nodded. "I have to do something to pay for our keep until your father returns. I have only a few coins left," she reminded him.

The upstairs rooms were furnished with beds to rent out, and, except for a musty, closed-up smell, these rooms seemed to be in better shape than the ones on the floor below. But the third story was the best of all. An apartment with a sitting room and two small bedrooms took up the whole floor. Although the rooms were stuffy and stale, the furnishings were passable enough.

Mrs. Bowden put Ben down on a small braided rug and sank wearily into an overstuffed chair in the sitting room. "It will be a lot of work, but I think we can make it. We'll live here on the third floor, and I can rent some rooms and serve meals. I will need your help, though. What do you say?"

"It's awful," Emma moaned. "I hate it here."

"Would you rather go to the poorhouse?" Thomas asked her fiercely. He turned to his mother. "I'll help you."

Emma hung her head. "I will, too, Mama."

"Good," Mrs. Bowden said briskly. "Thomas,

bring me a bucket of water. And look for some soap. We are going to need a lot."

The next few days were a whirl of scrubbing, sweeping, and hauling water. The linens were washed and hung in the garden to dry. Thomas scoured the pots with sand until they were shiny and bright. Mrs. Bowden washed the floors and the walls and polished the tables. Each evening, she spread a coating of glue on strips of paper and left them on the stove and kitchen floor. The next morning, they would carry out the strips, which were covered with bugs that had become trapped during the night.

One evening, Mrs. Bowden studied the account books she had found in an old desk. She laid out the few remaining coins and looked at them with a frown.

Thomas was making copies of a handbill to pass out. They advertised the new inn, and Thomas was writing each one carefully by hand. He searched the desk for more paper.

Emma had been given the job of watching Ben. "Now that Ben is crawling, he is into everything," she complained, following her little brother as he cheerfully skittered around the room.

"I wonder why babies crawl like that," Thomas said as he watched his brother.

"Their legs are not strong enough to walk," answered Mrs. Bowden.

"But why?" Thomas insisted. "Horses and cows can run as soon as they are born."

"It's just the way of things, Thomas," answered his mother. "Other creatures are born helpless." She pointed to old Nobbin, who was lying patiently while Ben pulled on his ears. "Dog and cats and mice are blind and weak when they are born." She smiled. "I see trouble has not changed your curiosity. As soon as things are settled, we must see about sending you to school."

Thomas, still searching through the desk, pulled out a piece of paper. His eyes widened. "Look at this."

Mrs. Bowden read quickly, a smile spreading across her face.

"What is it?" Emma demanded.

"It is a receipt for a case of rum and another of

cider. Rachel ordered it months ago. It is to be picked up on the docks. A place called the Lion's Head Importers and Exporters. With this, I think we can make it."

Just at that moment, there was a knock on the door. "Tell whoever it is that we are not yet ready for business," Mrs. Bowden said. Thomas hurried down the stairs to answer. But it was not a customer who stood there. To his surprise, it was the Jessups' servant, Lottie.

"Miss Lottie!" he exclaimed. "What are you doing here?"

"I heard you were going to reopen the inn. I brought my nephew to fix your sign. You can't have a respectable business with a falling sign," she said.

A tall young man was already unloading a ladder from the wagon.

"It's Miss Lottie," Thomas told his mother.

Mrs. Bowden invited the older woman inside, and they were soon talking like old friends over a cup of coffee. Miss Lottie reached under her shawl. "I almost forgot," she said as she handed Mrs. Bowden a folded paper. "A man brought this letter for you," she said. "Luckily, I got it and not the Jessups."

Mrs. Bowden took the letter. "A man?" she asked.

Miss Lottie shook her head. "A rather scruffy sort. He had a straggly beard and wore woodsman's clothing."

"Sam Tucker," Emma and Thomas chorused, remembering their friend's promise to contact Mr. Bowden. "Open it," Emma begged.

Eagerly, Mrs. Bowden broke the wax seal. "It is from your father," she said joyfully. " 'To my beloved family,' " she read out loud. " 'Word has come of your terrible ordeal. I grieve that I was not there to help you. I have learned from a messenger sent to General Washington that you made it to Stroudsburg and are headed for your sister Rachel's house. Next spring, my enlistment will be finished and I will join you there. God keep you until then.' "

"But we are not there." Thomas exclaimed. "How will father find us when he does come?"

"Don't you worry about that. I told your friend Sam where you were. He said he would relay that information as soon as he could," Miss Lottie said. She looked about with an admiring glance. "You've done wonders already. But I don't believe one person can manage an inn. I am not afraid of hard work."

Mrs. Bowden shook her head sadly. "I can't afford to pay you," she said.

"I'll work for board and room," said Miss Lottie. "One of those rooms upstairs will do nicely. When the inn is up and running, you can pay me seventy-five cents a day." Miss Lottie hesitated. "Mrs. Jessup figured out that I told you about this place. She's making my life miserable. So," she added with a twinkle, "you owe it to me."

"What if I don't get enough business?" Mrs. Bowden asked weakly.

"You will," Miss Lottie declared. "Most of the inns around here are dirty and noisy. Your children told me that you are a good cook. So am I. We'll tell people that this is the place to enjoy a good meal and quiet conversation at a fair price."

She patted Mrs. Bowden on the shoulder. "If they don't come willingly, we'll go out on the street and drag them in," she said with a chuckle.

For the first time since Mr. Bowden had left to join General Washington's army, Mrs. Bowden looked happy. "We'll do it," she said, shaking Miss Lottie's hand. She giggled, sounding for a second like a schoolgirl. "Won't your father be surprised?" she asked Thomas. "He left us to take care of a farm and he'll come back to find us running the best inn in Philadelphia."

"He'll be proud of you," Thomas said. "I know I am."

"I am, too," Emma said.

Their mother hugged them both. "How can I fail with you two to help me?"

FOUR

A Strange Encounter

Miss Lottie returned early the next morning with a small satchel of her belongings. Mrs. Bowden helped her move into one of the second-floor rooms. It was small, but a window overlooked the pretty yard in the back. As soon as she was settled, she helped Mrs. Bowden scrub all the windows in the inn with vinegar until they sparkled. The two put out the freshly washed linens and a small vase of roses on each table. The kitchen was gleaming and the serving room was warm and inviting.

"I think we are ready," Mrs. Bowden said, inspecting everything one last time. She sent Thomas and Emma with Miss Lottie to the big covered market near Christ Church to buy meat and fresh vegetables for the first meal.

Thomas was interested in the carpenters who were busily working with hammers and saws, repairing the stalls. "The British stabled their horses in the marketplace," Miss Lottie said indignantly. "They nearly destroyed it." She stopped to admire the fresh wood panels. "It will soon be better than it was before."

"Look at all this food!" Emma exclaimed as they wandered through the stalls. Farmers were selling fresh vegetables, pork, and poultry. Miss Lottie selected several freshly killed chickens, carrots, potatoes, flour, sugar, salt, and yeast. "When the British were here, nearly all the fresh food went to their soldiers. It was hard for ordinary citizens to find enough to eat," she said as they gathered up their purchases and headed home.

As soon as they returned, Mrs. Bowden mixed up several batches of bread and set them to rise in a sunny window. Emma helped Miss Lottie peel peaches from their very own tree to make into peach cobbler for dessert.

In the afternoon, Miss Lottie's nephew Jim arrived with his wagon to drive Thomas to the wharf to pick up the cider and rum. On the way, they passed out Thomas's carefully printed handbills. The sturdy mare pulling the wagon had been brushed until she gleamed. "I like your horse," Thomas said.

"Her name is Fancy," Jim answered proudly. "The redcoats took almost all the horses when they left, but they didn't take her. I rubbed Fancy with mud and tangled her mane and tail. They thought she was an old nag." He laughed out loud, obviously pleased at the trick he had played on the British.

"Why are so many of the warehouses along the wharves closed?" Thomas asked as they passed the boarded-up buildings.

"Tories owned them. They left with the British, and good riddance to them," Jim said darkly. "I hope your Lion's Head Importers is not one of them."

"No, there it is," Thomas said, sighing with relief.

Although the sign was large and showed a fierce lion in a toothy roar, the shop was a run-down unpainted wooden building. A little bell tinkled when Thomas entered the shop. The man inside was potbellied and had a narrow, pinched face. He seemed surprised when Thomas walked in. He glanced nervously toward a back room before he studied Thomas's paper with a scowl. "Thought you'd come before this. I ought to charge you for the storage."

Thomas was reluctant to tell him the truth. "We misplaced the receipt, and only just found it," he said after a moment. "We knew we could not get the rum and cider without proof that the bill had been paid."

The shopkeeper stared at him. "And right you were about that." He jerked his thumb toward two large crates beside the front door. Thomas looked around curiously. This was not like any store he had ever seen. Most of the goods seemed to be in crates. He could see even more boxes through the door to the back room.

"What are you looking at?" the shopkeeper said. "I told you your cider is over there."

"Sorry," Thomas said.

Jim helped him carry the first crate to the wagon. The surly proprietor watched, never offering to help.

"Not a very friendly sort, is he?" Jim muttered under his breath to Thomas.

"I never saw a store without goods on display," Thomas said.

Jim shrugged. "I suppose importers buy things for other shop owners to sell."

"He kept looking in that back room like he was worried we'd see something," Thomas said.

"Well, it's none of our affair," Jim said. They returned to the shop and Jim shouldered the second crate. Thomas opened the door for him. Just as he did, a rather large man rushed by, nearly knocking Thomas over. The man was clean-shaven, although he wore the long buckskin shirt of a backwoodsman.

"Watch where you're going," the man growled. Before Thomas could apologize, the man closed the door. Thomas stared after him. His clothes seemed out of place in the city. He hadn't gotten a close look at the man's face. Still, there was something familiar about him. Thomas was almost sure he'd seen him before.

As they climbed back in the wagon, Thomas heard the click of a lock. The proprietor put a sign in his window saying that he was closed, then pulled a dirty curtain over the window.

Thomas looked back at the shop, trying to think where he might have seen that man. Then he shrugged and put it out of his mind. He had enough to worry about. He crossed his fingers, hoping that customers would come to the inn. His mother had given Miss Lottie the last of the coins for the market. If tonight wasn't a success, he didn't know what they would do.

As soon as dusk settled over the city, Thomas saw that his worries were needless. Men started pouring into the little inn. Some came alone, some in boisterous groups of three and four. They ate, smacking their lips at Mrs. Bowden's good cooking, especially the peach cobbler, and stayed to talk

over a mug of cider or rum. Thomas and Emma scurried about all evening, wiping tables, taking orders, and washing the dishes first in a bucket of water and soap heated on the stove and then in one with clean water to rinse.

The ordinary seamen, who were known for their wild ways and brawls, frequented the inns closer to the wharves. The customers at the Peach Tree Inn seemed to be mostly sea captains and businessmen and an occasional army officer in a blue uniform from the detachment of soldiers General Washington had left to guard the city. Mrs. Bowden even managed to rent two of the beds to traveling salesmen from Boston, who seemed pleased at the clean, fresh-smelling sheets and newly scrubbed rooms.

Mrs. Bowden and Lottie collected coins in a small tin they had set out for that purpose. At the end of the evening, they looked in amazement at the pile of coins overflowing the tin. Even Thomas's pockets were bulging with pennies from customers who had sent him for fresh glasses of cider or rum.

When the last guest had departed, Thomas sat down at one of the tables, every inch of him exhausted. Emma had long since taken Ben upstairs to bed and fallen asleep herself. "Let her sleep," Mrs. Bowden had told Thomas when he had gone upstairs to see why she had not returned. "The poor thing is worn-out."

"I'll wager you never worked this hard at Mrs. Jessup's house," Mrs. Bowden told Miss Lottie.

"Never," said the woman. Then with a grin she added, "And never have I enjoyed hard work so much."

"I don't know what we would have done without you," Mrs. Bowden said warmly, "and your nephew."

A smile lit the old woman's face. "Well now," she said briskly. "Tomorrow, we will have to buy more food at the market stalls. If one more person had ordered dinner, we would not have been able to feed him."

While Thomas helped clean the tables, he listened to Miss Lottie talking to his mother about the British occupation of the city. "Just about every family had British soldiers living in their homes," she said. "Most of them were gentlemen. But some made the home owners act as servants to them." Miss Lottie shook her head. "All the time they were living in comfort, our soldiers were only twenty miles away, living in tents and crude huts at Valley Forge. Our poor soldiers were cold and hungry, and Congress didn't give them enough money for food, let alone warm clothes. The British blockaded the ports to keep out trade goods from the West Indies and patrolled every road leading out of the city."

"I suppose General Washington knows what he's doing," said Mrs. Bowden. "But I wish he had sent the army to help us when we were attacked."

"Maybe then we could have defeated the Tories and killed every one of the Indians, too," Thomas blurted out.

"Some people in Philadelphia say the Iroquois have reason to hate us. We have stolen their land and our diseases have killed hundreds of them," Miss Lottie said.

"They're murdering savages," Thomas said. "They don't deserve to live."

Mrs. Bowden looked at Thomas. "It is late," she said gently. "Hurry to bed before you fall asleep."

Thomas knew there were still pots and pans to wash and linens to scrub, but he was too tired to care. Slowly, he dragged himself to the third-story rooms and, without even bothering to undress, fell into his bed.

FIVE

School at Last

Sunlight streaming into the windows woke Thomas the next morning. He sat up and groaned. His arms ached from carrying the heavy tubs of water the night before.

Emma was playing with Ben in the sitting room. Since Ben was crawling now, he had to be watched every minute. He gurgled happily, seeing Thomas.

"Hello, Ben," Thomas said. He squatted down beside the baby.

"You missed breakfast," Emma said. "I ate hours

ago. Mama has a surprise for you," she added importantly.

Thomas stood up. "What is it?" he asked.

"You'll find out," Emma teased.

Thomas ran down the two flights of stairs. His mother was folding linens when he got downstairs. She looked up and smiled. "Good morning, sleepy." She dished him up a bowl of porridge. "It is cold, I'm afraid."

"I don't mind," Thomas said.

Mrs. Bowden sat at the table while he ate. "I've decided to put away a portion of the money each day for your aunt Rachel and uncle Charles. After all, it is really their inn."

"That's a good idea." Thomas nodded absently. He took a bite of his cold porridge and swallowed. "Emma says you have a surprise."

Mrs. Bowden nodded. "There is a school very near here. I'm going to enroll you children tomorrow."

Thomas jumped up, excited and happy. Even though his mother had taught him to read and their neighbor Mr. Hailey had kept him supplied with books, there was so much more he wanted to learn.

That evening, the inn was again busy. Word of Mrs. Bowden's good cooking had already spread through the waterfront area. Mrs. Bowden sent both Thomas and Emma to bed early. "It won't do to fall asleep your first day of school," she said firmly when they protested that she needed help. "Miss Lottie and I can manage."

The next morning, they arose before daybreak. Mrs. Bowden walked the few blocks with them to register for school. It was a large brick building that might have been someone's home at one time. At the door, a boy about Thomas's age gave them a curious look, then directed them to Miss Pettipoint's office. She was the headmistress of the school. Thomas sniffed the air with pleasure, liking the good smell of books and paper and ink.

Miss Pettipoint was a very tall lady, and so thin that Thomas wondered if she ever ate. Her gaze was direct and stern. She sighed when she learned that the two new students had never attended school before.

"They will have to go in with the primary students until they learn how to read," she said firmly. "The other students will tease, but it can't be helped."

"My children know how to read," Mrs. Bowden protested. "I've taught them at home. Thomas does especially well."

The headmistress peered over her spectacles with an owlish look. She handed Thomas a small book. It was written in simple rhymes. "This is very easy," Thomas said, reading several pages aloud.

The headmistress handed him several books, each slightly harder, but all easy for Thomas. "Well," she said, her voice friendlier. "Just what have you been reading?"

Thomas listed some of the books Mr. Hailey had lent him. "I've read most of Mr. Shakespeare's works," he said. "My favorite, though, is *Robinson Crusoe.* Mr. Hailey lent me *Gulliver's Travels,* but I didn't get to read it. The book was lost when the Tories burned our house."

"We will have to remedy that," said Miss Pettipoint. She handed a book to Emma and listened while she read. "You are both excellent readers," she said.

"I would truly like to learn the why of things," Thomas added helpfully.

Miss Pettipoint looked confused. *"The Why of Things*? I don't know that book."

"I mean why is the sky blue? And why is the moon round sometimes and not at others? Why is the earth flat in some places and there are mountains in others? Why do the trees turn red in autumn and lose their leaves? And why—" Suddenly aware of Miss Pettipoint's amused look, he fell silent.

"I believe I will put you in Mr. March's room. He teaches the fifth grade, and he, too, is interested in the 'why of things,' as you say," said Miss Pettipoint. "And are you interested in all these things, too, Emma?" she asked kindly.

Emma nodded. "Not as much as Thomas. But I would like to meet a friend."

Miss Pettipoint actually smiled. "We will see what we can do about that, too. I'm going to put you in our fourth grade. Your teacher will be Miss Lambert."

Mrs. Bowden said good-bye and headed back to the inn. Miss Pettipoint led Emma to her classroom and came back for Thomas. He had been sure when he'd walked into the room that he would not like Miss Pettipoint at all. Instead, as they walked to his class, he found himself telling her about the inn and even how much he missed his father.

Unlike the usual bare classroom, Mr. March's had paintings of strange animals pinned to the wall, and in jars near the window were butterfly cocoons, strange plants with needlelike thorns, and some things that Thomas did not even recognize.

The day passed so quickly that Thomas was amazed when it was time to go home. Thomas and Emma walked back to the inn together. "How did you like it?" Thomas asked.

Emma sighed. "It was all right, I suppose. I don't much like doing sums."

"Mr. March is a real hero," Thomas bragged. "His feet were frostbitten at Valley Forge and he had to have three of his toes amputated. He uses a cane when he walks."

"Did he know Father?" Emma asked with a worried frown.

Thomas shook his head. "I asked him. He said there were eleven thousand soldiers there. He said everyone was too busy trying to stay warm and finding enough to eat to make friends."

"Poor Father," Emma said sadly.

Thomas nodded soberly. They walked in silence for a few minutes, each thinking about how terrible the winter had been for their father.

"Mr. March is interested in scientific matters," Thomas finally said. "He says we are living in an age where scientists are discovering new things every day. He says maybe one of his students will discover something important. I hope it is me."

"What would you discover?" Emma asked just as they reached the inn.

Thomas shrugged. "How can I tell you? I haven't discovered it yet."

Practical Emma shook her head. "I've wondered about that. How can someone discover something new unless they are looking for it?"

"I suppose sometimes they find it accidentally," Thomas said.

"But if you are not looking for it, and you find it accidentally, how do you know what it is?"

Thomas laughed. "I think you are starting to ask better questions than I do."

They paused before crossing the street to wait for a large wagon rumbling toward them. They could hear pitiful groans from inside the canvas tarp as the wagon bumped over the rough paving. Two soldiers in tattered blue uniforms sat on the back. One had a bandage around his head. The other had a bloody cloth tied around the stump of his leg. Emma gasped. "What if one of those men is Father?"

"Don't even think that," Thomas said fiercely. "Father is fine." But he watched with troubled eyes as the wagon turned the corner, heading toward the hospital. It seemed as though every time he began to put the war out of his mind, there was something new to remind him.

"Don't say anything about the wounded soldiers to Mama," he said. "It will just make her worry more."

Emma nodded. They had reached the inn, and old Nobbin was waiting beside the door. He jumped up when he saw them coming and his tail waved in joyful circles. Thomas and Emma stopped to give him a scratch on his head. "Poor Nobbin. He must be really lonely when we are gone all day," Emma said.

Mrs. Bowden and Miss Lottie were peeling potatoes for the evening meal. "Well, how was your first day of school?" Mrs. Bowden asked. Ben sat on the floor by his mother, playing with two cooking pots. Thomas picked him up and swung him around. Ben giggled with delight.

Thomas set Ben back down on the floor. His lips twitched as he tried to hide a smile. "I learned something scientific today."

"Already," said Mrs. Bowden. "Your father will be so proud when he comes home. What did you learn?"

"We learned about the kind of stones that are found in a river."

Mrs. Bowden looked confused. "But there are all different kinds."

Thomas shook his head. "These are always the same."

"It's one of his tricky riddles, Mama," Emma warned.

Thomas nodded. "Do you give up? *Wet* stones are found in rivers!" he answered, laughing at his own joke.

"I know one, too," Emma said. "My new friend Mary told me at lunchtime. What side of a dog has the most hair?"

Mrs. Bowden, Thomas, and Miss Lottie all looked at one another. "The outside," they answered at the same time.

SIX

---◆---

Spies!

The Peach Tree Inn continued to prosper. Aunt Rachel's share of coins, safely hidden behind a loose brick in the fireplace, grew to a tidy sum, and there was enough money for new coats and shoes for the coming winter. There was even enough to pay the taxes, so there was no chance that Mr. and Mrs. Jessup could get their hands on the inn. Except for worrying about their father, it was a good time for Thomas and Emma. The leaves on the tree by the porch changed from green to red and finally fell as the horror of the massacre faded from Thomas's mind, although he knew he would never forget completely.

The leaves made a delightful crunchy noise when Thomas and Emma walked to school. They scarcely had time to notice as autumn slipped away toward winter, because they were busy from the first light of dawn until they fell in bed, exhausted, long after dusk.

On Sundays the inn did not serve a meal, so, except for the occasional overnight guest, there was a chance to rest. After church, Thomas and Emma explored the city. Miss Lottie had lived there all her life. Sometimes she accompanied them. They peeked into shop windows and marveled over the wide city streets, paved in the center, with brick walkways on either side. On almost every corner, there was a four-sided glass lamp to light the night. Some of the glass had been broken, probably by boys throwing stones.

"Look at this!" Thomas exclaimed one day. On the side of a building was a poster. " 'There is an award of forty dollars for information on the dastardly evil person who is breaking the glass on the streetlamps,' " Thomas read.

Miss Lottie handed them each a bun she had purchased at one of the many bakeries in town. "That 'dastardly evil person' is probably a schoolboy with too much time on his hands," she said, shaking her head.

They walked along, munching on the sticky buns. Thomas thought he would never see all of Philadelphia. No matter which direction they walked, there was always something new to see.

"There's the statehouse building, where the Declaration of Independence was written. Some people are already calling it Independence Hall," Miss Lottie told them. "The British kept prisoners there during their occupation." A sad look passed over her gentle face. "A lot of the soldiers died here, and they just dug a pit nearby and buried them."

"Father doesn't even know that Ben can sit up now," Emma said that night as she watched Ben stacking some smooth wooden blocks that Jim had made for him.

Mrs. Bowden looked sad. "He is sacrificing much for his country," she remarked. "But perhaps it will not be long now. Benjamin Franklin has persuaded the French to help us."

The hours Thomas spent in school were the best time of day. Mr. March was an excellent teacher, and he seldom had to punish his students, as some of the other teachers did. Although Thomas suspected he was often in pain, Mr. March was unfailingly kind and cheerful. Thomas made friends with a few boys in his class, but he did not have time to see them outside of school. Each evening, he helped in the inn, clearing tables, serving meals, and washing stacks of dirty dishes. Mrs. Bowden had decided to hire a part-time serving girl so that he and Emma would have more time to study.

Thomas rather enjoyed waiting on the tables. The customers seldom talked to him, although occasionally one of them would give Thomas or Emma a penny for extra-good service. As he served the tables, Thomas heard snatches of conversation. From the sea captains and officers, he learned that the British still patrolled the mouth of the Delaware River, making it hard to get badly needed supplies. The colonists were using smaller, faster ships to escape the blockade. Thomas heard exciting stories of ships hiding in small bays and inlets and sneaking past the British under the cover of night.

From the businessmen, he heard conversation about the difficulties of producing guns and supplies for the army. There was plenty of iron—Pennsylvania had vast stores of coal and iron ore—but shipping was difficult because the mighty Iroquois Nation was helping the British. Then, too, there was a lack of skilled gunsmiths and steel mills to turn the ore into weapons.

The dinner one evening consisted of a fine slice of roast beef, potatoes, and cabbage. For dessert, his mother had made bread pudding spiced with cinnamon. The weather had turned cold and the hard frost had stripped the last of the red and gold leaves from the trees. Thomas laid a fire in the big stone fireplace, making the serving room cheery and warm. The inn was so crowded, some guests were forced to eat standing along the back wall.

Three men sat at a small corner table, lost in conversation. One wore a blue jacket with gold braid and a sea captain's hat. He was a regular customer, but tonight, Thomas recognized his companion as the proprietor of the Lion's Head. The third man's back was turned, and Thomas could not see his face. The table was stacked with dirty dishes from dinner. With a start, Thomas remembered that he had not brought them their dessert. He carried over three bowls of pudding. The men were so intent on their conversation that several seconds went by before they noticed him.

"I want to be paid. I filled my end of the bargain," the captain said.

"You'll have it when we deliver. But you know how closely the docks are watched. We'll have to—" The speaker suddenly looked up and saw Thomas.

Thomas gasped. It was the same man who'd nearly knocked him down that day at the Lion's Head. But what made him catch his breath was the fact that he recognized him. Now he knew why the man looked so familiar. Thomas was sure that he'd seen that same man wearing Tory green right before the massacre in the Wyoming Valley.

Thomas looked away quickly and tried to hide his alarm, but the man must have seen the recognition in his eyes. The merchant of the Lion's Head jumped up. He grabbed Thomas by the front of his shirt as the tray of puddings dropped with a clatter. "Are you spying on us? What did you hear?" he shouted fiercely.

He had spoken so loudly that all conversation suddenly stopped. The room was deathly silent.

"Please, sir," Thomas said, trying to look innocent. "I was just bringing you the desserts. I heard nothing."

Mrs. Bowden came from the kitchen, wiping her hands on her apron. "Is there a problem?" she asked.

The sea captain looked embarrassed. "My apologies, good woman. My companion thought the boy was listening to our conversation. It was a mistake. He was only bringing us our desserts."

While his mother cleaned up the spilled puddings, Thomas cleared the dishes from the table, trying not to look at the Tory soldier. Mrs. Bowden followed him into the kitchen as he carried the heavy tray.

"Were you eavesdropping?" she scolded.

Thomas opened his mouth to tell her and then closed it with a snap. What if he was wrong? It had been nearly four months since the massacre and he had caught only a brief glimpse of the man.

Miss Lottie came to his defense before he could answer. "The children have been running all evening. Most likely, those three are up to some kind of mischief. Captain Larson has a reputation for pirating."

"He's a pirate?" Emma gasped.

"So I have heard," answered Miss Lottie. "Best to stay clear of those three."

"My goodness, it is so late," said Mrs. Bowden. "Emma, check on your baby brother to see that he's still sleeping. Then do your schoolwork and go to bed yourself. Thomas, when you have finished cleaning up, you may go also."

Thomas took a cloth and wiped the tables. He had decided he would talk to his mother, tell her that he suspected the man was a Tory spy. He would wait until the customers were gone and she had time to sit down and listen. In the meantime, he stayed clear of the corner table, but several times when he glanced over, he caught the Tory soldier intently watching. He was glad to go back in the kitchen, where he could escape the man's gaze.

Thomas washed the few dishes that were left and stacked them for the next day. He peeked back out in the serving room and was relieved to see that the man and his companions had gone. Miss Lottie and his mother were still in the front, tending to the last few stragglers. He tugged the heavy tubful of dirty dishwater outside and set it on the edge of the porch.

Suddenly, a large hand covered his mouth and he felt the hard barrel of a pistol against his back. A low voice whispered in his ear, "If you want to live to see tomorrow, don't make a sound."

SEVEN

Kidnapped!

Thomas nodded to show he understood. Slowly, the hand released him and Thomas turned to face his attacker. "You're a spy," Thomas sputtered.

The Tory soldier kept his pistol pointed at Thomas. "You were in the Wyoming Valley, weren't you?"

"So were you," said Thomas. "Killing your own countrymen."

The man's eyes glittered in the moonlight. He suddenly pulled up his shirt. "You see that?"

Thomas gasped. "It looks like burn scars."

"Burns, yes. That's what my countrymen did to me. My friends and neighbors burned down my house. Tarred and feathered me. And what was my crime? I'll tell you," he said when Thomas shook his head. "My crime was that I wanted to remain loyal to our rightful authorities."

Thomas gulped. "They shouldn't have done that to you. Even so, it didn't give you the right to murder people."

"I murdered no one," the soldier said. "I belonged to the Tory army. We fought a battle and we won."

"The Indians with you tortured people," Thomas hissed. "I heard them screaming."

The soldier looked away, his face pale. "That was unfortunate, but I had no control over anything that happened that night. The problem is what to do now. I can't risk your giving me away until my mission is done."

"Thomas?" called Mrs. Bowden from the kitchen.

The Tory grabbed Thomas's arm and pulled him into the bushes. "Not a sound," he reminded him.

Thomas's mother opened the door and looked out. "That boy," she said. "He took the tub outside and forgot to empty it before he went to bed."

"He was pretty tired," Miss Lottie's voice answered. "I'll help you dump it."

Together, the two women tipped over the dirty water. It flooded over Thomas's shoes as he stood only a few feet away. Thomas did not want to endanger his mother and Miss Lottie. He remained quiet, as the soldier had ordered. In a minute, Thomas thought with satisfaction, Mother will go upstairs and discover that I'm not there. She will raise an alarm, perhaps even waken the two Continental army officers asleep on the second floor. A second later, his hopes were dashed.

"I'd like a nice cup of hot chocolate," he heard Miss Lottie say as the door closed. "Shall I make you one, too?"

"That sounds perfectly lovely," his mother answered.

The Tory stepped away from the protective darkness of the shrubs. He motioned with his pistol, and, reluctantly, Thomas circled the inn to the street in front.

Thomas looked around for someone to help him, but at this late hour the streets were nearly deserted. It was cold, and Thomas shivered without a coat.

The soldier fell into step beside him, holding the pistol so it could not be seen by anyone walking by. Now that he had captured Thomas, he seemed almost sorry.

"Look, boy—Thomas, is it? I know you've had a bad enough time in this war. But you see my problem. They hang spies, and I am rather fond of my neck just the way it is."

"What are you going to do with me?" Thomas asked.

The Tory hesitated. "I don't know." He took off his coat and offered it to Thomas, but Thomas stubbornly refused. With a shrug, the soldier put it on again. He touched Thomas's shoulder. "Listen, we're leaving tomorrow. We'll just take you with us, and when we get far enough away, we'll turn you loose and you can make your way back home. By that time we'll be back with our own people, and no one will really have been hurt."

Was the "we" the sea captain and the owner of

the Lion's Head? Thomas wondered. Or were there others? By this time, they had followed the road nearly to the wharves. Thomas was so cold, his body felt numb. The Tory pointed to the familiar LION'S HEAD IMPORTERS AND EXPORTERS sign. "It will be warmer inside," he said as he unlocked the door.

Inside the building, it was not much warmer than outside. The Tory lit a lantern and directed Thomas to the back room. The room was sparsely furnished with a small cot covered by a dirty blanket, a table and chair, and a stove in one corner. Boxes and crates were stacked in every corner. "Wrap that blanket around you," the soldier said, not unkindly. He laid the pistol on the table and set about starting a fire.

Thomas eyed the gun, wondering if he could reach it and overpower the soldier. As though he had read Thomas's thoughts, the Tory picked it up and pointed it at Thomas. "I consider myself a good person. I do not consider myself a fool. If you keep your mouth shut and cooperate, you'll be heading home in a few days. If not, I won't hesitate to kill you."

Thomas curled up on the cot and wrapped the blanket around him. Tears of frustration stung at his eyes, but in anger, he brushed them away. He wouldn't let the Tory see how afraid he was. Perhaps the man would keep his word and let him go. But why was he here in the first place? It had to be something pretty important to risk his life. Thomas eyed the boxes and crates and thought about the bits of conversation he had overheard at the sea captain's table. Suddenly, he sat straight up. He knew what his captor was doing. He was taking supplies to the Tory army!

The man looked at him curiously and Thomas forced himself to look away from the crates. There must be some way to keep the shipment from reaching its destination. But how?

He pretended to close his eyes but left them open a tiny slit, enough to watch the soldier through his eyelashes. The man sat down in one of the chairs by the table as though he was waiting for someone. Once again, he laid the gun on the table, but this time he kept his hand nearby. The minutes ticked slowly by. The room was warmer now, and under the blanket, Thomas stopped shivering as the cold numbness subsided. It was hard to hold his eyes open. He let them close, promising himself that it was only for a minute.

He awoke to the sound of arguing and for a few seconds could not remember where he was. Then he sat up quickly, wondering how long he'd been asleep. The room was pitch-black; nevertheless, he had a sense that it was morning.

He swung his feet off the cot and stood up. Slowly shuffling forward, he held his hands straight out, looking for the door.

It was locked, but, when he tried the knob, the voices stopped. A second later, the Tory opened the door. Thomas stumbled out into the light.

To his surprise, the front room was nearly empty. Two brawny men were carrying the last of the boxes outside, where they were being loaded onto large wagons. The men started emptying the room he'd just occupied. He could see through the dirty window that it was almost dawn. The skies were gray and dismal.

The proprietor of the Lion's Head gave him a

sour look. "Don't give us any trouble, boy. If I had my way, you'd be lying in some alley with your throat cut. And maybe that mother and sister of yours, too. Give us a problem, and it still could happen."

"Leave the boy alone," the Tory said, stepping between them.

The importer shrugged. "Suit yourself. I say you are asking for trouble." He went outside, slamming the door as he left.

The Tory watched him go, frowning. Then he turned back to Thomas. "You are going to ride with me. My name is John Anderson," said the Tory. "And you are my son Thomas. We are loyal patriots on our way to the village of Easton to deliver this load of supplies to General Sullivan. He's gathering an army to reclaim the Wyoming Valley."

"I won't help you steal supplies meant for General Sullivan," Thomas said boldly.

"I am not asking you to help. But if you want to live, you will do as I say," Anderson replied. He handed Thomas a cup of hot chocolate and a bun.

"Take my advice and eat this. It may be awhile before there is anything else." He stared at Thomas. "Another thing. You are not to talk to anyone but me. Not even the drivers. Is that understood?"

Reluctantly, Thomas nodded. While he ate, one of the men he'd seen loading boxes came to the door and handed Anderson a package.

"We're nearly ready," he said.

Anderson nodded. He unwrapped the package and handed Thomas a warm coat. "Put this on," he said, "and take the blanket."

Thomas gulped the last of his cocoa and put on the coat. The Lion's Head proprietor came back in the building. He didn't speak, but he watched Thomas's every move. Anderson seemed a decent-enough person, but not so this man. Thomas knew that if he made one wrong move, the man would not hesitate to kill him. And if Thomas was reading his evil look correctly, the man would enjoy doing it.

EIGHT

———— ◆ ————

The Journey North

Thomas's small hope of escaping disappeared when he walked outside. There were six wagons, loaded and ready. Each was so huge, Thomas was reminded of a boat with wheels. The bottom of each wagon was painted blue, and the upper part was red. Each was topped with a skeleton of wooden ribs, over which was stretched white canvas. Both the front and back ends were slanted up. Thomas guessed it was to keep goods from sliding out in mountainous country.

Each wagon was pulled by six of the biggest horses Thomas had ever seen. They stamped their feet, impatient to be off, and their breath made puffs of white steam in the frosty air.

It was not the wagons that dismayed Thomas. Somehow, he had imagined that he and the man who called himself John Anderson would make the journey with only a few others. That might have made escape possible. Now he realized that he would be traveling with a small army. In addition to the driver, three or four men, out of sight and heavily armed, rode inside each wagon. Several others walked alongside the wagons, and behind them all was a smaller cook wagon with food and supplies.

Anderson held tightly to Thomas's arm, guiding him to one of the wagons. "Stay with me," he said. The Tory looked at his partner from the Lion's Head with a wary eye. "You'll be safer," he added.

Reluctantly, Thomas climbed into one of the wagons, as he was directed. Several long, flat boxes stacked on one end made a long bench. He sat down and looked at the stacks of blankets and boots that filled most of the wagon. With winter closing in, they would help keep the enemy warm. Thomas wearily pulled his own blanket around his shoulders. The canvas cut out some of the wind, but it was still freezing.

From the driver's seat, John Anderson looked back at Thomas as the wagons rolled out of the city. "These are Conestoga wagons," he said in a conversational tone. "They can hold ten tons of goods. The horses are specially bred to pull heavy loads."

A few minutes later, they reached the outskirts of the city. "Get up here quickly," Anderson hissed.

Thomas scrambled to the front and climbed on the seat next to Anderson. "There's a checkpoint ahead. Remember, you are my son. They would not believe I would take my son if it were anything more than a simple delivery." He gave Thomas a hard look. "Don't try anything funny. If the guards at the checkpoint suspect anything, we will have to kill them."

Anderson pulled in the reins and the wagon stopped. A Continental soldier in a clean blue uniform inspected the papers Anderson handed him. "I was at Valley Forge last winter," the soldier remarked. "We could have used supplies like this then."

"I heard it was terrible," Anderson answered.

"Three thousand men died from the cold and hunger. Things are better now. Supplies like this help," the soldier said. He smiled at Thomas. "This is quite an adventure for you," he said.

"Were you really with General Washington?" Thomas asked.

Anderson's hand clamped around Thomas's arm in warning.

The soldier nodded. "He's a great man."

"My, uh, uncle was there," Thomas said, ignoring the threat. "James Bowden. Did you know him?"

The soldier shook his head. "Sorry, son. There were so many." He handed back the papers and waved them on.

"You did well," Anderson said as they rolled away. "That soldier is convinced we are patriots, with your uncle being at Valley Forge."

Thomas stared at him. How could he have been so stupid? Without meaning to, he had actually helped Anderson.

"I wasn't trying to help you," Thomas said bitterly. "I just didn't want you to shoot him."

Anderson sighed. "Get in the back," he said shortly. "I didn't want to shoot him, either," he added as Thomas closed the canvas flap.

The wagons passed through several other checkpoints during the day. Thomas was careful not to speak again. The surrounding countryside was settled with prosperous-looking farms and several small settlements. But by evening, the farms were farther apart and there was less traffic on the road.

They stopped for the night in a quiet meadow. Thomas was determined to make his escape. He was pretty sure he could make it back to the last checkpoint in a couple of hours. He watched for his chance all evening while the soldiers set up camp, but none came. Anderson fetched him a plate of salt pork and beans from the cook wagon. With a warning not to move, he allowed Thomas to sit on a log while he ate.

Whenever Anderson was not with Thomas, the proprietor of the Lion's Head was never more than a few feet away, watching menacingly. His name was Arthur Davis, Thomas had learned. Thomas feared him more with each passing hour. While Thomas ate, Davis talked to Anderson. Thomas knew they were talking about him from the way Davis looked at him several times as he spoke. Anderson shook his head violently. "No," he shouted once. "I won't have it."

The salt pork churned uneasily in his stomach. Anderson had shown no sign of turning him loose as he had promised. Were they going to kill him after all? Thomas forced himself to continue eating. If he did escape, he would have a long walk before he reached his next meal.

Anderson jumped up and walked away without looking at Thomas. Davis, however, gave him a triumphant smirk before he followed Anderson. Thomas put down the tin plate and pulled the blanket around him. Trying to look casual, he studied the camp, looking desperately for some means to escape.

The soldiers had erected a large tent. The wagons had been drawn into a half circle around the tent and strips of canvas were fastened around their bottoms to break the wind so that some of the men could sleep underneath. They were camped on a high bluff overlooking the river. There was no escape that way, Thomas knew. This time of year, the water was dark and cold. Without a boat, it would be impossible to cross it.

A drop of rain splashed on him, and he looked up at the sky. Thick black clouds boiled over the camp. Another drop of rain hit him, then another.

The rain came down harder, and the soldiers started storing away the supplies. Anderson was near the tent, directing the men as they scurried about. Davis was nowhere in sight. For the moment at least, everyone seemed to have forgotten about him. Thomas stood up. Under the cover of the pelting rain, he furtively backed toward the circle of wagons. Slowly, he inched his way between two of the wagons. Most of the soldiers had retreated to the canvas-protected underside of the wagons and were already curled up in their sleeping rolls. A few were still repacking the cook wagon. They were intent on their work. Quickly, Thomas slipped between the wagons, intending to make a run across the meadow.

"Going somewhere?" said a hated voice. Davis grabbed a handful of Thomas's hair and dragged him back inside the circle. Still holding his hair, he yanked Thomas to the tent. Then he lifted the flap and shoved Thomas roughly inside. Thomas stumbled and fell to the dirt floor. Davis had pulled his hair so hard that Thomas's head burned and his eyes watered.

"He was trying to escape," Davis said. "I told you we should kill him."

Thomas's mouth was dry with fear. Anderson looked pained. "I will take care of him," he told Davis.

"Didn't do a very good job of it before," Davis said. He took a long, wickedly sharp knife from a sheath he had fastened to his belt. He slowly picked at his fingernails with the sharp point, all the time watching Thomas with unblinking eyes.

"You should not have tried to escape," Anderson

said. His voice was no longer kind. He took a length of rope and roughly bound Thomas's hands together. He fastened the other end around his own wrist. Then he threw a blanket on the ground and motioned for him to lie down. Without speaking again, Anderson stretched out on a sleeping roll beside him. Davis watched for a few minutes before putting his knife away and blowing out the candle. Thomas heard Davis mumble to himself and groan as he settled in his own sleeping roll on the other side of Thomas.

Thomas was too frightened to move. He stared in the darkness until the soft, even breath of sleep came from both sides. At last he allowed himself to relax.

The ropes chafed on his wrists and his clothes were soaked from the rain. Thomas shifted uncomfortably. He tried to wrap the blanket around himself and was rewarded with a sharp reproof from the Tory.

It was a long, miserable night. The rain continued, tapping gently on the tent canvas. Thomas could not sleep. He thought of the comfortable inn and his family. His mother must be frantic by now. And Emma. Even though they teased and argued, Thomas missed her terribly.

It seemed as though Thomas had barely fallen asleep when he was awakened by the sharp poke of a boot. "Get up," Davis growled. Anderson had freed himself, but Thomas's hands were still tied and his fingers were numb. Anderson cut the rope. Thomas shook his hands, trying to get the feeling back. Anderson pointed to the cook wagon. "Get something to eat," he said roughly.

Under Anderson's watchful eye, Thomas stumbled over to the cook wagon, slipping and sliding on the muddy ground. He sipped the cup of watery coffee the cook gave him and chewed a soggy biscuit while he watched the men break camp.

The men's mood matched the weather. There were curses as they harnessed the horses, and several loud arguments. In spite of this, camp was quickly broken and in a few minutes they were on the road again. Thomas sat back down on the long boxes in Anderson's wagon. He wondered what was in them. Suddenly, he stood and stared at the

crates. There could be only one thing in crates of that size. Guns. Blankets and boots were bad enough. But each one of the guns could kill settlers. He sat down again and looked hopelessly out of the back of the wagon as they rolled farther and farther from his home.

NINE

Another Patriot

In spite of the early start, they did not make much progress. Even in good weather, the wagons were slow, but now the rain had made the roads almost impassable. The wheels sank into the ruts, sometimes burying the axles. The horses groaned with the effort to free the Conestogas. Several times, Thomas was required to push at the back with the other men while the drivers snapped their whips. Sometimes a wagon would be freed, only to become stuck again a few feet farther on.

By afternoon, they had gone only two or three miles. Thomas had not felt well all day and now he was sneezing and his head felt hot. When he coughed, his chest ached. They passed a small grassy meadow, and after a hasty conference Davis and Anderson ordered the wagons to stop for the night. The cook, a friendly man with leathery skin from working outdoors, handed him a plate of salt pork and boiled potatoes. Thomas choked down a few bites and set his plate down on the ground. He sat on the stump of a tree, listlessly holding his head in his hands.

"You're not eating," Anderson said. He peered at Thomas with a concerned look on his face. "What is the trouble?" He felt Thomas's head and muttered an oath. "You are burning with fever," he said.

He motioned to two of the men who were watching curiously. "My son is sick," he said. "Re-arrange boxes in that wagon so he has a warm bed."

Thomas waited while the men did as they were told. Sick as he was, he took note of the fact that

Anderson was keeping up the charade in front of his men. That must mean that at least some of the men were not in on the plot. No wonder Anderson had ordered him not to talk to any of them. He studied their faces, wondering which ones were not involved.

As soon as a spot had been arranged, Anderson led Thomas to the wagon and covered him with an extra blanket. In spite of that, Thomas shivered so hard his teeth rattled. His throat burned like fire and his ribs ached from coughing. Just before dark, the cook came to the wagon. Anderson watched while he rubbed salve on Thomas's chest. Despite its foul smell, the salve felt warm and comforting.

"You'll feel better tomorrow," Anderson promised. He leaned back on a pile of blankets, keeping watch.

Thomas did not improve during the night. In the morning, his fever raged and he could hardly breathe unless he was propped up in a sitting position. Things seemed fuzzy and not quite real. After breakfast, which Thomas could not eat, the wagons continued on their bumpy way. Thomas was tossed about in his makeshift bed, but he was too sick to care. Once, he thought an angel was there, and he felt the cool touch of a gentle hand on his head. When he opened his eyes, he saw it was only Jake, the cook, come to rub more foul-smelling salve on his chest. He was so disappointed, he could not stop the tears that ran helplessly down his cheeks.

"Here, now," the cook said kindly, "it's not as bad as all that. My salve will fix you up before you know it."

The next days passed by in a blur. Thomas scarcely knew night from day. He thought they crossed a river once, loading the wagons onto large rafts and floating them across. Then for a time they seemed to be in the mountains. He heard the ring of axes, widening the trail in spots where it was too narrow for the awkward wagons. Then there were shouts and whistles as the men urged the horses over the steep terrain. One morning, in a brief moment of clearheadedness, he thought he smelled smoke. He crawled over to the opening of the wagon and lifted the canvas flap. He saw a cluster of burned cabins. The fire was recent. Thin trails of smoke rose from the blackened shell of what had once been someone's home. There was a bundle of rags near the charred remains of a doorway. It took Thomas a moment to realize he was looking at a body. Rage clutched at his heart. By the clothes, he knew it was a woman, but her head was bloody and her hair was gone.

Gasping in horror, he let the canvas close and crawled back to his bed. The wagons stopped for a time while the men dug a pit and buried the dead.

Thomas realized he had no idea where he was. He had even lost track of how many days they had traveled. Sick at heart, he closed his eyes and went back to sleep.

That night when Anderson came, Thomas was awake. He realized his cough was better and he was hungry.

Anderson seemed pleased. "You've been pretty sick," he said. "I wasn't sure for a while that you were going to make it."

"As if you cared," Thomas snorted. His voice cracked weakly when he spoke.

Anderson turned away. "I'll get Jake to bring you some broth." He jumped down from the wagon. Then he turned back. "I'm not a monster, you know."

Anderson returned with the cook a few minutes later. Jake watched while Thomas eagerly drank the soup. "I knew my salve would heal you," he said proudly.

There was the sound of shouting near one of the other wagons. Anderson hurried away to investigate. Jake peeked out of the tent. "Looks like two of the men are fighting," he said.

"I remember you taking care of me," Thomas said. He smiled through lips that were cracked from fever. "I thank you. I thought you were an angel once."

"Weren't nothing, boy," Jake said, looking embarrassed.

Thomas looked out the opening in the canvas. "Where are we?"

Jake shrugged. "New York. We should be meeting General Sullivan's men any day."

Thomas struggled to sit up. Could it be that Jake

was one of the men who didn't know of the plot? He decided to take the chance. "General Sullivan is in Easton, Pennsylvania," he croaked. "He's gathering an army to retake the Wyoming Valley."

Jake chuckled. "That fever has scrambled up your mind. Why would we come all the way to New York if he was right there in Easton?"

"Because these supplies are going to the Tories," Thomas said quickly. "Anderson is not my father. He kidnapped me. He and Davis are Tor—" Thomas did not finish his sentence. The canvas flap was suddenly thrown back and Davis stood there glowering.

"If the boy is well enough to talk, he doesn't need any more coddling," he said. His eyes flicked suspiciously from Thomas to the cook. "What's he talking about, anyway?"

Jake chuckled. "I think the fever has rattled his brain," he said. Thomas's heart sank. Jake had not believed him. But Jake's next words gave Thomas hope. "He says he thought there was an angel rubbing some foul-smelling salve on his chest. That's the first time anyone mistook me for an angel."

Davis's scowl relaxed. "You better take care of the men. I'll watch the boy."

Thomas did not speak to Davis. He watched through the flap as Jake made his way to the cook wagon. Several times he stopped and spoke a few words to one of the soldiers and then walked on. After a few minutes, each man got up and sauntered casually over to the cook wagon.

Thomas tried to contain his excitement. Jake had believed him. Davis was still staring at him. "I'm really tired," Thomas said at last. "I think I will go to sleep."

"Good idea," Davis said. Still, he made no attempt to leave.

Thomas closed his eyes. He was tired. He knew he would never escape now. He was just too weak from the sickness to make such a long journey, especially with winter settling in. What was even worse was that he had no idea where he was. His one chance of getting home was for Jake and his men to take over the wagons and deliver them to the patriots. Thinking this, he fell into a troubled sleep.

TEN

Attack!

Thomas woke to the sounds of gunfire and shouts. It was still dark; only a hint of dawn glowed on the horizon. Thomas sat up, trying to make sense of what he was hearing. Peeking out of the canvas, he saw dark shapes moving and the sudden flash of a musket. "Over there," he heard someone shout. It sounded like Jake, and he allowed himself a moment of fierce joy. Jake and the rest of the men must be trying to take over the wagons.

He jumped up from his pallet, but his legs trembled and he was forced to sit back down. In spite of the battle raging around him, he discovered that his main thoughts were about food. He had been sick for over a week, he figured, and during that time he had had only a few sips of soup.

He tried to follow the battle from the sound of gunshots and the shouts and curses of the men. There was a smattering of fire from near the first wagon. Someone raced by the wagon, but Thomas could not see who it was.

There was a loud cry from the woods surrounding the camp and another farther away. At the same instant, a bullet tore through the canvas right over his head. There was an answering shot from inside the camp and a short scream as the bullet found its mark. Suddenly, the sounds of gunfire increased to a steady roar. The gunfire seemed to come from everywhere. Thomas flattened himself between several boxes, listening to the fighting and trying to decide what to do. If he could get to Jake, maybe he could help. He was a good shot with a musket.

There was a brief lull in the shooting. Thomas

worked his way to the back of the wagon and cautiously peeked out. There was a man lying on the ground only a few feet away. Thomas recognized him as one of the wagon drivers. He was dead and a pool of blood was slowly being soaked up in the frozen earth.

Thomas could see figures running through the trees and hear an occasional burst of gunfire. The cook wagon was perhaps twenty feet away, but there was no sign of life around it. The whole camp, in fact, seemed deserted. Quietly, Thomas crawled over the edge of the wagon and dropped to the ground.

The effort exhausted him. His head seemed to spin, and he forced himself to stand up. He reached out a hand to steady himself against the wagon. The sight before his eyes made him suck in his breath in horror.

There were scores of soldiers dressed in the hated green jackets of the Tory army surrounding the wagons. There were Indians with them, fierce warriors with painted faces and scalp locks. Thomas was frozen in terror. For an instant, no one moved. Then with an ear-piercing yell, one of the Indians leapt between two wagons and raced straight toward Thomas. Thomas did not even have time to run. The warrior's face, painted black on one side, was fearsome. It was twisted in a grimace of hate. He ran to Thomas, a tomahawk raised in one arm.

Suddenly, a second warrior stepped between them and gave a sharp command. The first man stared defiantly for a second. Then he slowly lowered the tomahawk and stalked back to the waiting soldiers.

Thomas fought to keep his knees from shaking. He wasn't sure why he had been spared. Then a cold feeling crept over him and he swallowed. He remembered the screams of the captured soldiers after the Wyoming Valley massacre. It would have been better if the warrior had killed him outright. The Iroquois tortured their prisoners. His savior was watching him. Thomas forced himself to stand tall and face him, although his stomach churned with fear.

There was approval in the warrior's eyes. He

reached into a pouch tied around his waist with a leather thong. Thomas shrank back as the warrior reached toward him. The warrior's fingers were covered with a red dye. He made a mark on Thomas's forehead. "You must be brave. My friend Anderson has told me about you, little brother. I have made my mark on you so that none will harm you," he said in perfect English.

Thomas felt his mouth drop open in surprise. Before he could gather his wits, the Tory soldiers burst into the circle of wagons. Flushed with victory, they scrambled over the wagons, harnessing the horses and preparing to leave. Thomas saw John Anderson at last, leading a defeated group of men out of the woods. Their hands were tied in front of them and some were bloody from wounds. There were Indians with them. The warriors poked and prodded their prisoners into the circle of wagons. The men huddled together, defeated and fearful, while their captors whooped and shouted gleefully. Several of the warriors waved fresh scalps that were still dripping blood.

"Jake," Thomas shouted, spotting the cook

among the captives. Jake managed a weak smile. "I was worried I'd wasted all my special salve for nothing."

"I'm all right," Thomas said. He saw blood on Jake's shirt. "You're hurt."

"It's only a little nick on my arm," Jake said. "Just our bad luck we tried to take back the wagons right when the Tory soldiers appeared."

"I shouldn't have told you," Thomas said. "It's my fault this happened."

Jake shook his head. "They would have captured us anyway. This way, at least we took a few of them down," he said, smiling grimly.

John Anderson waved his pistol at Jake. "Quiet," he ordered.

Thomas turned to John Anderson. "What are you doing with those men?" he demanded.

"They won't be harmed. We are taking them to Fort Niagara," Anderson answered. "We'll use them to trade for some of our men."

"Is that what you are going to do with me?" Thomas asked weakly. His body swayed and he feared he would faint if he didn't sit down.

"We still have a long ways to go," Anderson said. "With you alive, Davis can never go back to his import business. I don't think you would survive the rest of the trip." He pointed to the tall Indian who had made his mark on Thomas. "There is a Mohawk village nearby. He will take you there."

Fear made his mouth dry. "You are giving me to the savages?" Thomas gasped. "Kill me now. At least I won't be tortured."

Anderson nodded to the tall man standing quietly by Thomas. "This is Thayendanegea. Most people call him by his English name, Joseph Brant. He has promised to take you to a safe place," Anderson said.

"How can you trust the word of a savage?" Thomas asked desperately. "He will kill me."

Although Thomas knew Joseph Brant understood the conversation, the Indian's face remained emotionless.

"I know him as an honorable man," Anderson said, sounding impatient. "You will not be harmed. Unless you do something foolish," he added.

Thomas looked at the warrior. "I've heard of you. People say you were there—at the massacre."

"I was not there," Brant said mildly.

Thomas ran after Anderson. "You promised to let me go," he begged. "Let me walk home."

Anderson roughly pushed him aside. "Enough of this! It's winter and you are hundreds of miles away from Philadelphia. You wouldn't survive two days out there by yourself. I am saving your life, even if you don't believe it. You are going with Brant, and that is the end of it."

ELEVEN

———— ◆ ————

Joseph Brant

The Tory detachment stayed only long enough to harness the horses and bury the few men who had been killed in the skirmish. The road was still slippery, but less so than earlier in the day. By midday, the last wagon was out of sight. Thomas had to fight the urge to run, screaming, after the wagons. No matter what Anderson had said, Joseph Brant was feared all over the frontier. People called him "Monster Brant."

The tall Indian had not spoken again. He sat

with four other warriors around a small fire, talking quietly in their own language. Now and then, he glanced at Thomas, who was huddled, miserable and cold, on a log, his blanket clutched around his shoulders. At last, they seemed to have reached some sort of agreement. They stood up and kicked dirt over the fire. Joseph Brant motioned to Thomas. "You come with us now."

They set off at a quick pace through the woods. They followed a trail that rose sharply, then twisted through spaces so treacherous and narrow that they had to walk single file. Thomas stumbled and fell, and the warrior walking behind him spoke sharply and reached for his tomahawk. A cruel smile crossed his pockmarked face. Thomas had seen such disfigurement before, on the Indians in their valley who had survived smallpox.

Joseph Brant held up his hand. He paused only long enough for Thomas to scramble to his feet. "You must keep up," he said softly.

The warriors seemed nervous. They spoke little and often looked back, as though they feared they would be followed. At dusk, they stopped for the night at a crude lean-to made of bark.

It was bitterly cold and a light dusting of snow covered the ground, but at least there was some protection from the wind. Two of the warriors gathered firewood and soon had a good fire burning. Thomas squatted as close as he dared. He stared at the fresh scalps the warriors had tied to the thongs around their waists. The pock-marked warrior had the most. Thomas counted six. Brant handed the boy a lump of food from his pack. It seemed to be made of cornmeal, grease, and dried berries. It was tasteless and gritty, but surprisingly filling. One of the men filled a pot from a nearby stream and set it in the coals to boil. Later, when it had cooled, they passed it around, each man taking a few sips. When it was handed to Thomas, he was surprised that it was tea.

When the fire had died down to coals, a blanket was fastened over the open side of the lean-to. Although the ground was hard and cold, the heat of their bodies and the coals kept them comfortably warm. The smoke made Thomas cough. He rolled up in his blanket and tried to sleep.

In the morning, he was feverish and his body was stiff and sore. He was offered some more of the greasy cornmeal mixture, and, as before, it filled his stomach. While he chewed, he thought of his mother's hotcakes, dripping with butter and maple syrup and served with chunks of fried ham. He forced himself to stop thinking of home, because it made him feel too sad. He didn't think he could make it through another day of traveling, but he was sure the pockmarked warrior would kill him if he did not keep up. He concentrated on taking one step, then another. The land was difficult, with deep ravines and sharply rising hills that were thickly forested. Often their way was blocked by fallen timber. They stopped only once, near a clear, fast-moving stream, where they drank and rested a few minutes, then continued on their way without eating. As the day passed, the warriors became less uneasy. Their pace relaxed, and they even joked among themselves.

Thomas could feel his fever getting worse. The sickness had returned, worse than ever. He could feel the fever burning behind his eyes, yet his body shivered and his teeth chattered with cold. He coughed so much, his ribs ached. He plodded along, trying to keep up, but he was falling behind with every step. Late in the afternoon, Brant dropped behind him, and Thomas knew he was ready to kill him for being so slow. Thomas prayed it would be quick. But Brant reached out with a steady arm when he faltered. "It is not far now," he said.

Thomas found the courage to ask, "Why do you speak our language so well?"

"I was educated at a white man's school," Brant answered. "I have even been to England," he added. He touched a heavy metal collar around his neck. Thomas saw that it was engraved with an English crest.

Thomas fell silent. Joseph Brant spoke perfect English and his voice was that of a cultured gentleman. But his body and face were painted with black stripes and markings. His head was shaved on the sides, so that only a narrow strip of hair remained in the middle. Over the scalp lock, he wore a small cap of turkey feathers.

By late in the day, the trees had gradually thinned out. They were on a gently sloping hill, and Thomas could see a wide valley below them. A clear, swift river twisted and looped through the valley like a carelessly thrown ribbon. He could see in the distance a village surrounded by acres of cornfields. The warriors talked and laughed, eager to get home. Their pleasure was so great that when Thomas stumbled again, the pock-faced warrior waited without anger, even though Thomas was slow to rise.

The trail wound past the cornfield. Most of the corn had been picked, but here and there Thomas saw fat orange squashes growing on vines between the dry stalks. Beyond the cornfields was a small orchard of peach and plum trees. Thomas was amazed at the size of the cornfields and orchards. How did those people he thought of as savages keep such vast fields under cultivation?

At last, he had a clear view of the village, and

Thomas allowed himself a moment of hope. Perhaps the Indians were taking him to his own people after all. The town had been built close to a bend in the swift-flowing river. There was one long bark-covered structure with a rounded roof close to the river. It was too big to be a house, and Thomas guessed it might be a meetinghouse of some kind. The rest of the town was a cluster of comfortable-looking cabins, much like his own home on the frontier before the Tories had burned it.

Something was strange about the houses. None of them had chimneys. Instead, smoke rose from a small hole in the roof. He had been mistaken. This was an Indian village after all.

Thomas's disappointment was so great that he sank to his knees and could not force himself to rise again. Brant was beside him instantly. Gripping Thomas beneath his arms, he hauled him to his feet again. Thomas staggered after Brant until they stopped in front of one of the cabins. It was made of logs neatly fitted together. Mud and grass had been stuffed in the cracks to keep out the cold. A thin plume of smoke rose from the roof.

It seemed as though the whole town had turned out to see them. A crowd was gathering, mostly women and children. They greeted Brant and his companions with happy shouts and laughter, all the while eyeing Thomas with curiosity.

Thomas shrank back in fear, but Brant nudged him gently toward the house. The inside was sharp with the smell of wood fire, but except for the fire in the center of the room, it was not unlike those of his own people. Brant spoke in his language to a woman who sat in one corner on a small wooden bench.

While they spoke, Thomas looked about the cabin. Along one wall were wide benches. Reed mats were neatly rolled up at one end, and Thomas guessed they were for sleeping. In one corner were woven baskets of various sizes, obviously used for storage, and there was an assortment of clay pots stacked near the cooking area. The floor was dirt, but there were several richly colored mats to brighten up the room.

"Thomas," Brant called. Reluctantly, Thomas went and stood beside him. "This is Laughs-at-Rain. You will stay with her. I have business away from here."

Laughs-at-Rain touched Thomas's face and arm and hair. Thomas shrank back in horror. Was she thinking of scalping him as soon as Brant was gone? The woman said something to Brant. Her voice was musical and soft.

"She says you are very handsome for a white boy," Brant said. Laughs-at-Rain's hand touched Thomas's face and her voice changed. She spoke rapidly in her own tongue to Brant, who answered back.

"Now what is she saying?" Thomas asked suspiciously.

"She is concerned that you have a fever. I told her that you have been sick."

Brant started to go. Then he turned back to Thomas. "Laughs-at-Rain got her name because she was always happy. But the American soldiers killed her husband and older son. Another son died of the disease you call measles, so she no longer laughs."

"Wait," Thomas called. "If the Americans killed her family, she will hate me. She probably wants to kill me."

Brant paused. "Laughs-at-Rain had no son. Now she does."

TWELVE

Steam Bath

Thomas swayed slightly. What had Brant meant? How could he be this woman's son? I have a mother, he wanted to scream.

Laughs-at-Rain unrolled one of the sleeping mats and motioned for him to lie down. He was too exhausted to do anything but obey. He watched as she busied herself with the clay pots at the fireplace. He thought of his own mother, busy in the kitchen at the inn. Perhaps now he could escape. Surely it would not be too difficult with only one tiny Indian woman to guard him. But he was far away from home, deep into the Indian lands. Even if he did manage to get away, how could he avoid capture by other Indians, perhaps less kind than Brant and Laughs-at-Rain? And even if he did get away, how would he feed himself? He had no weapon. On top of that, winter was near. That afternoon, he had seen what looked like snow clouds in the sky.

For now, he might be better off staying where he was. Brant had said he was to be Laughs-at-Rain's son. He had heard of Indians adopting white people. Sometimes when the captives were rescued, they did not want to return to their own people. That would never happen to him, he was sure. He hated these people. He would wait until the proper time and slip away. Still thinking this, he fell asleep.

It was morning when he awoke. His head hurt and he groaned slightly as he struggled to sit up. Sometime during the night, his new "mother" had covered him with a soft deerskin robe. It was cold in the cabin, and he wrapped it around himself as he got up.

Laughs-at-Rain was stirring something in a clay pot over the fire. She smiled broadly, offering him a steaming cup.

He sniffed it suspiciously. It had a strange spicy smell and he was reluctant to drink. Laughs-at-Rain nodded and smiled. Then when he still seemed reluctant, she poured some for herself.

He took a sip and gasped. It was hot, not just from the fire but from the spices. Still, it was a pleasant taste, so he drank some more.

When he had finished his drink, Laughs-at-Rain pulled a soft shirt and leggings out of one of the baskets and next to them she laid a beautiful pair of moccasins with a bright design sewn on for decoration. She pointed to his shirt and pants and showed him with gestures that he was to take them off.

Thomas looked down at his clothes. They were dirty and little more than rags. Even so, he was reluctant to part with them. He shook his head, but Laughs-at-Rain reached for his shirt and started to pull it off. He shrank back and reluctantly took off the shirt himself. He reached for the new shirt, but she shook her head and pointed to his pants. Thomas clutched his pants and shook his head.

Laughs-at-Rain leaned close and sniffed. Then she held her nose and made a face. Again she pointed to his pants.

Thomas was embarrassed. There was no doubt that she was telling him that he smelled. But smelly or no, he was not going to take off his pants with her standing there. He looked around for something like the big tin tub he bathed in at home, but he saw nothing that looked like it was used for that purpose. He shook his head, harder this time, making her giggle. He wasn't sure if it was the sickness or the drink, but he felt light-headed and his body was flushed. He swayed slightly, gripping a post to keep from falling.

Laughs-at-Rain picked up the steaming pot and motioned him to the door. Thomas was completely mystified, but he followed her.

It was freezing outside, and his arms were immediately covered with goose bumps. Laughs-at-Rain set a quick pace toward the river. Thomas tried to quiet the panic he felt. Was she taking him to be tortured? He had heard of settlers who were burned at the stake or even skinned alive. As they crossed the village, Laughs-at-Rain stopped several times to talk to other women. They smiled and nodded approvingly. Thomas stood stiffly while the women talked. He saw a few old men and several boys about his own age heading in the same direction. Were they all going to watch? He saw very few warriors. Maybe they are all out attacking settlers, he thought bitterly.

They reached a small bark-covered hut close to the river. An old woman tended a fire outside the hut. A pile of stones, each about the size of a turnip, was in the middle of the fire. Thomas felt his knees turn to water. He was right. They were going to torture him.

The other boys and men wore only breechcloths. It was cold, but it didn't seem to bother them. The younger boys looked curious. They stared at Thomas, who was shivering with fear and the cold. One of them said something, and they all laughed. Thomas flushed. He was sure they were laughing at him. The men's faces remained expressionless. Several of them slipped into the hut, carrying kettles of drink like the one Laughs-at-Rain had brought with them.

Thomas was overcome with a fit of coughing. Laughs-at-Rain said something in her own language. She handed the kettle to Thomas and pointed to the door. A deerskin flap covered the doorway, so Thomas could not see inside. Steeling himself against what was to come, he lifted the flap and entered.

It took a minute for his eyes to adjust to the dark. It was hot, steamy hot, and he saw that the steam rose from several large pots of water. A low bench was along the back wall. One of the boys pointed to a vacant spot on the bench. He took his place beside several of the other boys, weak with relief. Perhaps this was some sort of strange ritual. It did feel good. His goose bumps disappeared, and after a while he began to relax. He watched the other boys and sipped his drink when they did. He was warm inside and out. Beads of sweat dripped down his back. Every few minutes, the old woman tending the fire came in and placed more hot stones in the pot.

There were two boys who were close to his own age. One of them scowled at Thomas. He was tall and quiet, not joining in when the other boys jostled and poked one another with elbows and knees. The other boy was shorter. His black eyes sparkled with mischief. He pointed to himself and said a name Thomas could not pronounce. The boy took a stick and drew a beaver in the dirt. Thomas recognized the big front teeth. "Beaver," said Thomas. The boy nodded. "Beaver," the boy said, pointing to himself. Then he drew a small beaver beside the first. Thomas stared at the drawing. He snapped his finger. "I understand," he said. "Your name is Little Beaver." He pointed to himself. "Thomas."

One of the men suddenly spoke. The two boys stood up and motioned for Thomas to follow them

outside. Reluctantly, he obeyed. It was pleasant inside the steam hut.

Once outside, he looked for Laughs-at-Rain, but
she was not in sight. He stood uncertainly, watching the other boys. Then Little Beaver took his arm
and tugged him toward the riverbank. "Thomas,"
he said, pointing to the water.

Two older boys raced out of the hut and
plunged into the freezing water with a whoop. The
taller boy motioned for Thomas to jump in, too.
When Thomas shook his head, the boy gave him
a scornful look. Without warning, he shoved Thomas so hard that he lost his balance and fell into
the river.

Thomas gasped in shock at the icy water. Several
other boys, including Little Beaver, jumped in,
splashing him again as he tried to climb out.
Shrieking with laughter, the boys jumped out of
the water nearly as fast as they'd gone in. Thomas
scrambled after them. They raced back for the hut,
pulling Thomas along with them. The tall boy
stalked after them, continuing to glare. Thomas's
teeth chattered from the cold. His trousers clung

to him, feeling cold and clammy. The boys laughed, making their teeth chatter and pointing at him. Thomas managed a weak smile as the steam warmed him.

Twice more, the boys plunged into the icy water and then ran back to the hut. Each time, Thomas objected, but the boys laughingly pushed him in. When they went outside for the third time, Laughs-at-Rain was waiting. Her skin was glowing and her hair was wet, and Thomas wondered if the women had a similar steam bath farther up the creek. She wrapped a deerskin robe around his shoulders and they hurried back to the cabin. Laughs-at-Rain handed him his new clothes. Hiding under the robe, he quickly dressed. The clothes were soft and comfortable. The moccasins were a little big, but they were lined with warm, soft fur. Thomas wondered how Laughs-at-Rain could have known what size clothes he needed. Then he understood. These had belonged to the son who had died from measles.

Thomas realized that he felt better. His headache was gone, and though he still had a cough, even it seemed better. He was also starving. He eagerly ate the food she gave him. There was smoked fish, a fried bread made of corn, and a drink made from berries.

Laughs-at-Rain felt his head. This time he did not shrink away. She smiled and nodded. Whether it was because Thomas had allowed her to touch him or because his fever was gone, he didn't know. As she busied herself about the cabin, she pointed to objects, naming them. She made Thomas repeat the words until he could say them correctly. Then he taught her the American word for the object. Laughs-at-Rain giggled each time she made a mistake, and after a while he found himself laughing with her.

As the days went by, Laughs-at-Rain allowed Thomas to walk around the village. With words and gestures, she let him know that the longhouse he had noticed the day he arrived was the council meetinghouse.

Thomas thought of nothing but escape. He was never alone and there never seemed to be an opportunity. Then it was too late. A week after he arrived, a storm blanketed the village with nearly two feet of snow.

THIRTEEN

A Time for Learning

The day after the snowstorm, Thomas was helping Laughs-at-Rain gather firewood, when he saw Little Beaver. Strapped around each of his winter moccasins was a strange flat woven board. Thomas was curious. He had never seen anything like them. They seemed to be made for walking in snow. Thomas pointed to the snowshoes. Little Beaver took one off to show Thomas. It was made of a bent piece of ash netted with deer-hide thongs.

Little Beaver grinned as he walked with them back to the cabin. After Thomas dropped his stack of firewood by the door, Little Beaver took off the snowshoes and gave them to Thomas to wear. As Thomas practiced walking outside the cabin, Little Beaver and Laughs-at-Rain stood in the doorway, laughing at his first clumsy efforts. Thomas was amazed. Wearing the snowshoes, he could walk across the snow without sinking in. With snowshoes, he might be able to escape, even if the ground was covered with snow. Reluctantly, he took the shoes off and handed them back to Little Beaver.

Little Beaver talked earnestly to Laughs-at-Rain. She looked worried, and Thomas knew she still did not trust him out of her sight. At last, she nodded. From a storage basket, she pulled out an identical pair of snowshoes and handed them to Thomas.

His new friend motioned for him to follow. They walked the same path Thomas had traveled on when he first came to the village.

At last, they arrived at a bare hillside. Several other boys were there, including the sour-faced boy who had pushed him into the river after the steam bath. Using woven reed mats, the boys were sliding down the hill. Little Beaver reached under his robe and pulled out two thin mats. He handed one to Thomas and they raced to the top with the others. So many boys had come down the hill that the sliding area was like ice and was difficult to climb.

At the top, Thomas spread his mat and sat down. The hill was so icy that his mat was moving before he had even settled. Instantly, he was flying down the hill. He let out an unrestrained whoop of joy like the others as the mat slid faster and faster. He came to an abrupt halt when he veered off into a high snowbank. Laughing, he stood up and brushed the snow from his face. An instant later, Little Beaver whizzed by, coming to a slower stop as the land flattened out near the cornfield.

The rest of the day passed in fun and laughter. Most of the other boys accepted Thomas. They seemed pleased that he had learned almost enough words to have a conversation. Not everyone was welcoming, however. A few boys continued to stare at him with suspicion, including Hare, the boy from the steam bath.

Laughs-at-Rain was waiting by the door when they returned. A look of relief passed over her face when she saw him, and she smiled as she coaxed him near the fire to warm his hands and feet.

A group of hunters had returned that afternoon with several freshly killed deer. As soon as Thomas was warm, he walked with Laughs-at-Rain to the center of the village. In preparation for a feast, a huge bonfire had been built and the women were cooking the meat on spits made of forked branches. There was a festive air as the good smell of sizzling meat filled the air. Today at least, Thomas seemed to be an accepted part of the village. People smiled and greeted him, and for the first time, although he still desperately wanted to return home, he felt he was among friends.

As darkness fell, several men began to play on small drums made of deerskin stretched over a frame, and others shook rattles made from turtle shells with small rocks inside. Nearly the entire village stood up to dance. The dancers formed circles, with the men on the inside. They moved to the rhythm of the drums, although some of the young men leapt and twisted, showing off for the girls. The older girls pretended not to notice, but they prodded one another and giggled as the dancers twirled by. The women made up the outer circle. They danced more gracefully, patting their feet in time with the drums. They stood straight, with their arms hanging down at their sides.

Thomas sat on a log and watched. The music sounded strange at first, but after a time the melodies began to make sense and he tapped his feet, keeping time.

Then suddenly the music stopped, and the dancers sat down as a young warrior stood near the fire. He spoke too fast for Thomas to understand, but from the watchers' rapt attention, he guessed the man was telling a story. Suddenly, he raised his tomahawk. Attached to it were several scalps. One had the long blond hair of a girl. Another was soft and thin like that of a very young child.

Sickened, Thomas turned away. How could he have allowed himself to enjoy the day? How could he have forgotten he was the captive of savages? Even Little Beaver was listening to the story, clapping his hands in delight. Thomas stumbled back to the cabin. He would renew his efforts to escape. Even if he died out there in the woods, it would be better than living with the enemy.

For the next two days, Thomas stayed in the cabin, refusing even to go out with Little Beaver. Laughs-at-Rain watched him with a worried frown. He lay on his sleeping mat all day, with his back turned to her.

On the third day, Little Beaver came again. This time, he was with a tall warrior who had tattoos on his face and arms. Thomas knew enough words by now to understand that this was the boy's father, Dark Eagle. "Go," said Laughs-at-Rain, giving him no choice.

Dully, he walked behind Little Beaver and his father to a place on the river. Thomas saw large silvery fish swimming in the cold, clear water.

Little Beaver showed him how to use a fishhook fashioned from a dried bird's claw. With a net, they scooped up the silver fish and put them in a basket to take home. Not far away was a small handmade dam. A basket had been left on one side as a trap. Little Beaver pulled out several fat fish and showed Thomas how to reset the trap.

Laughs-at-Rain was delighted with Thomas's share of the fish. She cooked two of them that night and smoked the rest for later.

The winter days passed slowly, with snow so deep there was no chance to escape. It seemed that they did little but eat and sleep. Thomas thought longingly of the busy inn. He thought of the books Mr. Hailey had let him read just the winter before. Even if he had a book, he knew he would not have been able to read it. Without a chimney, the cabin was often filled with so much smoke, it made his eyes water.

Thomas spent hours talking with Laughs-at-Rain. He could speak her language almost perfectly, although she still chuckled occasionally when he used the wrong word. She told him the legends of her people, how long ago there had been five warring nations that had banded together to become the powerful Iroquois. Before the white men arrived, the Iroquois had lived in long bark-covered houses. Many families, all related to the oldest woman, shared a home. In fact, they had been called "People of the Longhouse." Now most of them lived much as their white neighbors did, although sometimes more than one family lived together. They talked about Joseph Brant, the war chief of the Iroquois League, the same Joseph Brant who had brought Thomas to the village months ago. He had once been a man of peace, even translating parts of the Bible into Mohawk. Laughs-at-Rain did not know where he was, but she knew he was fighting to help the British win the war. When Thomas tried to explain the horrors of the attack on his home along the Susquehanna, Laughs-at-Rain looked at him sternly. "That land was stolen from my people," she said in her language, and changed the talk to safer things.

At last it was spring. The people poured out of smoky cabins, eager to breathe fresh air. Women shook out sleeping mats and left them in the sun.

Before the snow completely melted, Thomas accompanied Laughs-at-Rain and the other women while they gathered sap in bark containers. They left it outside to freeze in the still-cold night air. The next morning, they chipped away the water that had risen to the top and frozen. They boiled what was left in large clay pots, stirring constantly. After a few hours, most of the syrup was divided, with some for each household. The rest was boiled until nothing but sugar crystals remained. This was divided also. The children gathered snow from the last shady nooks in the forests and their mothers sprinkled it with syrup. Laughs-at-Rain made some for Thomas. He smiled his thanks as he licked the tasty treat.

As the earth warmed the forest floor, it became dotted with spring flowers. Mountain laurel made the air smell sweet. The village did not have a medicine man with herbs and powders for healing, but each woman made some for her own house. Laughs-at-Rain took Thomas with her while she gathered trillium and special kinds of bark. When they returned home, she dried and ground the bark into powder. Mixed with water, it would heal small wounds and stop bleeding. Mixed with other ingredients, it made a poultice to stop coughs. From the trillium, she made medicine for headache and to cure itches and chapped hands. Everything was placed in pots and baskets and stored carefully under the benches where they slept.

Blossoms covered the trees in the orchard, and it was time to plant the three sisters: corn, beans, and squash. Planting was women's work, but rather than drudgery, it was a joyous occasion. The ground was prepared with tools made of bone and wood, and even some they had traded for from the white men. Then they brought out baskets of seed hoarded through the winter months. Some dropped the seeds in place, while others covered them with dirt and tamped them down. With so many hands, the tasks went quickly. They laughed and sang and admired fat babies born during the long winter.

While the women worked, the men jumped, wrestled, and ran races, gambling good-naturedly on the outcome. There was never anger from the losers. They smiled and thanked their opponents for the game.

Dark Eagle, Little Beaver's father, taught Thomas how to use a bow and arrow. Little Beaver watched, offering advice or laughing when Thomas missed the targets. Although Thomas liked Little Beaver, he kept his heart hard. He reminded himself that in a few short years Little Beaver, too, would be killing settlers. His only thought was of escape. He practiced intently, knowing these skills he learned would help him survive when he made his run for freedom. Perhaps Dark Eagle understood what was in his heart, because at the end of each lesson, he took away the bow and arrows.

One day, Thomas heard the warning shake of a rattlesnake lying nearby in the sun. He took aim with his arrow, but Little Beaver put a hand out to stop him. "We do not war with Grandfather Snake," he said as the creature glided silently away.

"My people always kill rattlesnakes," Thomas answered, speaking in the Mohawk language.

Dark Eagle spoke to Thomas. "When you make

war on rattlesnake, does he not sometimes attack you?"

Thomas nodded. "Sometimes people are bitten, yes."

"Then white people have only themselves to blame. They should stop their war with the snake," Dark Eagle said triumphantly.

One day, Thomas was allowed to leave the village with a small party of hunters, although he could not carry a weapon.

After walking a few miles, they came to a village. This one had many longhouses, like the one where the men sat in council in his own village. A wooden stockade still surrounded the village, but the houses had fallen into disrepair and it was plain no one had lived there for a long time.

"What happened to all the people?" Thomas asked, imagining it must have been a terrible disaster to make an entire town disappear.

Little Beaver shrugged. "That is Old Town," he said. "It is where I was born."

"But why does no one live here?"

"Mother Earth was tired. The corn grew smaller

ears and at last nothing grew at all. It is always so," Little Beaver said. "When Mother Earth no longer sends enough food to last the winter, we find a new place to live."

"How many Old Towns are there?" asked Thomas.

Little Beaver shrugged. "Many. My people have lived on this land since before anyone can remember. Now white men want to buy our land. We tell them man cannot own what belongs to everyone. The British say they will take no more, but the Americans trick us or steal what they want."

Trying to sound only curious, Thomas asked, "Are there Americans nearby, then?"

Little Beaver's smile disappeared. His eyes narrowed and he glared at Thomas. "You treat me as a fool. I know that you want to run away and break Laughs-at-Rain's heart. We have made you a friend. Be careful, Thomas, that you do not become our enemy."

FOURTEEN

The Hunt

In early summer, a small detachment of British soldiers rode into the village. While the soldiers set up a small camp, the officers met with the men in the long council house. Some of the women, Laughs-at-Rain included, were asked to sit in on the meeting.

The meeting lasted for hours. Thomas knew from Little Beaver that the meeting would start with the ceremonial passing of the pipe.

Sometime in the late afternoon, a British officer

set up a table in the center of the village. The men lined up, and as each approached the table the officer traded the scalps on each belt for money, knives, axes, and other goods. Each scalp was marked, Thomas learned, so that the officer could see at a glance whom the scalp had belonged to and how they had died. For example, if the skin was painted brown, the scalp had belonged to a farmer, and if it also had a small red foot, the man had died fighting. Less money was paid for the scalps of children and infants, and that of a fighting soldier brought the biggest price.

Thomas watched the proceedings with hate in his heart. That a British officer could sit calmly trading for the scalps of hundreds of men, women, and children made his stomach twist and boil with disgust. The officer held up a scalp with pale red hair and said something to the warrior. Both men laughed. Thomas could not watch any longer. He went inside the cabin, shaking with anger. Laughs-at-Rain brought him a clay bowl full of soup, but he only played with it. "You think we are savages because we take scalps. Yet the British pay for them, and they are not savages."

When Thomas didn't answer, she sighed. "We will lose in the end," she said sadly. "More and more settlers come all the time. They kill us with guns and they kill us with their sicknesses. And they kill us with strong drink that makes a man forget his pride."

Thomas turned away, refusing to listen.

Thomas knew it was time to leave. He had been planning it for weeks. He had a vague idea of walking south, following rivers whenever he could. He had put supplies in a carefully hidden deerskin bag—fishhooks, corn cakes, and dried fish, even the clothes he'd worn when he first came. The clothes would be too small—he'd grown since he'd been here—but he would wear them just the same. He watched Laughs-at-Rain, surprised at how sad it made him feel to leave her. She had been kind to him, and he knew his leaving would make her unhappy. He had to keep reminding himself that she was just a savage.

He intended to leave early in the morning. When he awoke, however, he saw that the British were still camped near the river. By the time they finally broke camp and rode away, it was too late. He would leave the next morning, he promised himself.

Laughs-at-Rain seemed unusually quiet all day, and several times Thomas caught her watching him. Did she somehow sense what he had planned? When she finally spoke, however, her words were unexpected.

"The men are going on a hunt tomorrow."

Thomas nodded, holding his breath.

"Dark Eagle asked if you could be trusted away from the village. I told him yes." Laughs-at-Rain paused, looking at Thomas.

Thomas understood. She had vouched for him and would lose face if he ran away. He nodded, his mouth dry.

Laughs-at-Rain seemed satisfied. "They will take you with them. Dark Eagle has given you this," she said, reaching under her sleeping mat. She handed Thomas a beautifully made bow and a handful of arrows.

Thomas gasped in delight. He ran his hands along the smooth curved wood of the bow. This would make his escape even easier. Then instantly he was overcome with guilt. By this gift, the people were saying they trusted him, and that Thomas had been accepted as one of them.

Thomas was up before the first rays of sun streaked across the horizon. Even so, Laughs-at-Rain was already stirring her pots, making his breakfast. She was full of advice. "Always thank the spirit of any animal you kill for allowing you to eat it," she reminded him. "Make sure none of the other hunters is in the way before you let your arrow go."

Thomas chuckled. He watched as she wrapped bread in leaves to stay fresh for later. Impulsively, he gave her a hug. He was surprised to find he could look her in the eye. He had grown since he came. The deerskin leggings were almost too short. "I will be all right," he said. "Don't worry."

"I have a gift, too," she said. She hung a quiver round his neck to hold his arrows. The thongs were long enough to go around his neck and under his left arm, so that the quiver hung at just the right place at his side to grab an arrow quickly. Laughs-at-Rain had made the quiver of soft deerskin. On the front was an eagle sewn with dyed porcupine quills. Thomas had seen her working on it through the winter months. "It's beautiful," he said with delight.

The eastern sky was just starting to glow when he stepped outside. He felt a burst of pride. Last time, he had only been a tagalong. Now he would take his place among the hunters.

There were ten grown men and five younger boys in addition to Thomas. A few of the older warriors stayed home to protect the village.

The hunting party walked single file along one of the many trails through the woods. Late in the afternoon, they stopped beside a stream to drink. Thomas knelt by the stream and cupped water in his hands. Suddenly, he froze. There in the wet mud at the edge of the stream was the biggest footprint he had ever seen. "Bear tracks!" he yelled.

The hunters rushed over to examine the tracks. One of them sniffed the dirt. "Not long ago," he said. Another pointed farther up the stream. "Two cubs with her."

The hunters were excited. "You have done well," Big Hare told Thomas. The other boys looked envious that they had not been the first to see.

Steadily, the hunters followed the tracks. On the rocky ground there were none, but there were other signs—a bit of fur, a tree trunk scratched with deep grooves. Once as they climbed a hill, they caught sight of her in the distance. She was a huge bear with shaggy black fur.

At the sight of her, Thomas stepped up his pace, nervously keeping his hand near his new quiver, but the others called for him to slow down. "We will follow her until she is tired," Dark Eagle explained.

At dusk, they built a crude shelter that had a peeled-bark roof supported by four posts. They unrolled mats and sat on them to eat. Each hunter carried a small pouch. Inside was a paste made of cornmeal sweetened with maple syrup. Laughs-at-Rain had prepared one for Thomas. He ate some of it and found it was surprisingly tasty. Only a few bites made him feel full. After he ate, he slept soundly until morning.

He had imagined they would be up early and back at the hunt, but the sun was high before they set off again. An early-rising hunter had speared fish from a nearby stream. They wrapped the fish in green leaves and roasted them over hot coals. Together with another taste of the cornmeal, it made a satisfying meal.

It wasn't long before they saw fresh signs of the bear. The hunters discussed a plan. They were on a hill that had a high sheer bluff on one side. They would spread out, driving the bear to the cliff. Perhaps they would trap more game this way also. They spread out, making a wide circle. Thomas grabbed his bow tightly. His hand felt sweaty with excitement. When everyone had had time to get in place, they started the drive toward the cliff. The hunters yelled and screamed ferocious noises as they moved forward. Thomas tried to yell, but his mouth was dry and his yells sounded more like squawks.

The woods were suddenly alive with crashing

and pounding feet. Steadily moving forward, they pushed their prey toward the cliff.

Thomas had lost sight of Little Beaver. Looking through the woods, he could see the next warrior in line with him. He tried to match the pace. A deer suddenly broke lose and crashed through the trees only a few feet from Thomas. It was so fast, he didn't have time to raise his arrow. It bounded away to freedom. They were almost to the broad clearing in front of the cliff, and still there was no sign of the bear. Thomas tripped over some wild vines and almost fell, but he caught himself just in time. He heard a whimper high above him in a tree. He looked up and saw two small cubs peering down at him with bright eyes.

"I found the cubs," he shouted, wondering if he could be heard over the other hunters.

Suddenly, there was a sound that made his heart skip a beat. With an angry roar, the bear crashed through the trees less than ten feet away. The bear towered over him on her hind legs. He could smell the awful stench of her and see the saliva that dripped from her sharp teeth. Her claws were so large that Thomas knew one swipe would kill him. Moving slowly, he fitted the largest arrow in his bow and took aim.

If he missed, the bear would kill him before he had a chance at another arrow. He tried to see if any of the other hunters were near. He heard a tree limb breaking off to one side and saw Big Hare running to help. He is too far away, Thomas thought desperately.

Big Hare was yelling, distracting the bear. She roared another challenge. His arrow was ready, but Thomas held back, one second, two.... Then, from the tree, one of the cubs suddenly squealed for his mother. Instantly, the bear dropped down on all fours. In that same instant, Thomas let loose his arrow and ran. He heard an angry roar and the bear stumbling behind him. She moved fast for such a huge beast. Thomas heard a second arrow whiz though the air. Big Hare had found his mark.

The bear squealed again, but she did not stop. Thomas reached for a second arrow and fitted it as he ran. He could feel her hot breath behind him. She wheezed as though she was hurt, but she con-

tinued after him. Thomas whirled and shot without taking time to aim. The arrow buried itself deep in her neck. Again she rose on her hind legs. Thomas took a step backward and tripped over a root. With a strangled roar, the bear fell. Her body pinned Thomas's legs and her mighty head was in his lap. With a final shudder, she died. Thomas felt his head swim, and suddenly there was only darkness.

FIFTEEN

———•———

The Celebration

When Thomas opened his eyes a few minutes later, Little Beaver's joyous face hovered over him. "He's alive," his friend shouted happily. Dark Eagle's face came into view. "I think our great hunter only fainted." He chuckled. "Good thing you killed the bear first."

Thomas was embarrassed. He struggled to sit up. But the bear's weight held him down. From behind, one of the hunters grasped Thomas under his arms and pulled while several other men lifted up the bear.

Thomas scrambled to his feet. He was covered in sticky blood, but it all belonged to the bear. "Are you hurt?" asked Big Hare. He seemed relieved when Thomas shook his head. "Laughs-at-Rain would never forgive us if we let you get hurt on your first hunt."

"Thomas has a name," one of the boys shouted. "Man Who Holds Bear in Lap."

Thomas had to endure several minutes of teasing and laughter. The boys crowded around, punching and jostling one another. Thomas had to tell his story several times. He swaggered a little with pride.

Dark Eagle held up his arm. "We thank you, great bear spirit, for allowing us to kill you. There will be food for many nights for our people." Then he squatted and examined the bear. Several of the other hunters had shot their arrows, but it was Thomas's arrow in her neck that had finally killed her.

The men set about skinning and gutting the bear. Then meat was divided into sections and wrapped in fresh leaves for the journey back home. There was plenty for each man to carry, and they staggered under the weight. Big Hare showed Thomas the bear's long, curved claws. "This will make a fine necklace for you. Then all will know you as a mighty hunter."

A young hunter named Climbs Trees showed how he got his name. He scrambled up the tall tree and brought the squealing, wiggling cubs down one by one. One of the men fashioned leashes for them.

"What will they do with them?" Thomas asked.

"We will keep them in a pen until they are bigger," answered Little Beaver.

Thomas looked at the little cubs. They were cute now, but soon they would be just like their mother. Thomas knew how important bears were to the village. In addition to the meat, which was used for food and religious ceremonies, the bear grease was used in the summer to keep away flies. Laughs-at-Rain used it to keep her hair shiny and smooth. Thomas had gotten used to the smell of bear grease. White people often thought the Indians were dirty because of the smell. Now that he had lived with them, Thomas knew this wasn't true. Most of them bathed in the river nearly every day, and Laughs-at-Rain kept her cooking pots clean and the cabin tidy, just like his own mother.

The whole village turned out to greet them. In addition to the bear, the hunters had stumbled across a flock of young turkeys. They had managed to kill seven fine fat birds. Thomas's arrows had all missed, which brought even more teasing. "It's lucky you didn't shoot like that when the bear was coming after you," one hunter said, laughing.

"Thomas saves his arrows for big targets," said Big Hare.

Thomas laughed with them. "I had to let the rest of you catch something," he said.

The women took the meat to prepare, and arrangements were made for a feast. The smaller children ran after Thomas, begging to see the bear claws. He held them up and growled fiercely, making them run away in mock terror.

Laughs-at-Rain carefully tied each claw with a thin piece of deer-hide thong. Thomas put it around his neck, pleased at the way the claws curled around his chest.

At the feast that night, there was bear and turkey, fresh greens with nuts, and corn bread with berries.

When everyone was full, the storytelling began. Dark Eagle began with the story of Deganawidah, a healing spirit in human form who came to the great chief Hiawatha with the laws of peace. Thomas had heard the story many times from Laughs-at-Rain, but he listened intently as Dark Eagle told them again how Hiawatha had persuaded the chiefs of the Mohawk, Oneida, Cayuga, Seneca, and Onondaga peoples to join together to form the Iroquois League of Five Nations. "We are Mohawk, the keeper of the eastern door," Dark Eagle reminded them.

At last it was time for Thomas. He stood before them and recounted his adventure. He was careful not to sound too proud and to give the other hunters credit. He acted out the story, creeping along when they stalked the bear. He watched the younger children's eyes grow wide with imagining the hunt. Even the adults leaned forward, anticipating the moment when the bear would leap out of the brush. Thomas roared, shaking his necklace, and the audience gasped with fear and delight.

It was almost morning when mothers picked up their sleeping babies and gently prodded snoozing elders as everyone headed for their sleeping mats. The bear claws rested comfortably against Thomas's chest as he trudged beside Laughs-at-Rain, heading home. He was full, happy, and proud. He was also too tired to hold open his eyes.

SIXTEEN

—•—

Heading Home

The weather that year was the best anyone had ever seen. The sun made the corn grow tall, and when the rains came, they were gentle. Laughs-at-Rain picked berries with the other women, and what they did not eat, she spread on sheets of hide to dry.

Every day, Thomas planned his escape. And every day, he put it off for yet one more day. He spent most of his time with the other boys his own age. They wrestled and ran races and swam in the river. Dark Eagle taught him the duties of a man. He helped clear more fields for the women to plant, repaired Laughs-at-Rain's house, and even made a long bench for outside the door so that she could sit and talk with her friends when the work was done. The bearskin had been cured and now lay across his sleeping shelf. When visitors came, they spread it on the floor by the cooking fire for a soft place to sit.

A pen was built for the two cubs in the center of the village. The youngest children spent time every day finding grubs and berries for them to eat. Thomas didn't want to think about what would happen to them later. For now, the cubs seemed content tumbling about in the pen as they wrestled with each other.

When the corn was high, a runner came to the village with disturbing news. An army was approaching from the south. General Sullivan was on the move, and he was determined to burn every village from Pennsylvania to Canada and drive the Indians from their lands.

The men talked among themselves. "The British will help us," said Dark Eagle. "King George has said he is like our father. A father does not forget his faithful children. The Iroquois have helped the British soldiers; now they will help us."

Runners came with more bad news. "The war goes badly for the British. They cannot spare soldiers to help us."

That night, the fires burned late at the council house. When Laughs-at-Rain returned, she told him the decision. "There are too few of us left to fight an army. If they come, we will go north to join the rest of our people."

Her face looked suddenly old. "You have not been with us long enough. I know that you still long for your people. There are some in the council who do not trust you. The time has come for a choice. Will you come with us?"

Thomas touched her hands. "You are friends— no, more than friends. But I belong with my own people."

Laughs-at-Rain looked at him for a long time. At last, she nodded. She unrolled her sleeping mat. In a few minutes, her even breathing told Thomas she was asleep.

Thomas lay on his own mat, unable to sleep. If

he could find General Sullivan and his army, he might find a way to get home. He thought of how surprised his mother would be when he walked in the door. Emma would not believe how much he had grown. It was hours before he was finally able to fall asleep.

The sun shining on his face woke him the next morning. He stretched without opening his eyes. There was no welcoming smell of breakfast. "Laughs-at-Rain?" he called. He sat up, suddenly alarmed. It was quiet, too quiet. Nowhere in the village was there a dog barking, nor any of the morning sounds. He sat up slowly, with a growing feeling of dread. The fire was cold. Laughs-at-Rain's sleeping mat was gone, as was her carrying basket. Other than that, everything was in place.

He stumbled to the door and looked out. The village was empty. Only an eerie silence greeted his calls.

He went back inside and searched for something to eat. Sitting on his bear rug, he nibbled some smoked fish and corn cakes. He would wait for the army. They would help him get home. But why did he have such a feeling of dread? He thought of the people he had known in the village. Laughs-at-Rain, Little Beaver, Dark Eagle. Once they had been the enemy, but no longer. He could not believe they had left without even saying good-bye.

The army must be very close for the people to have deserted the village so quickly, leaving so much behind. Yet the morning dragged by, and still he was alone. The silence was unnerving. He went outside and walked around the village. The bear cubs were still in their cage. They bawled at him, asking for food. Thomas opened the gate. The cubs stood there, uncertain what to do.

"Go on," Thomas screamed. He picked up stones and threw them. The bear cubs still did not move. They squealed unhappily. Thomas charged at them, yelling and waving his arms. At last they turned and lumbered off into the forest. Thomas stared after them, wondering if they would survive.

He walked to the river and spent the morning exploring. In the afternoon, he thought he heard several large booms. He listened, but the sound did not repeat. Perhaps it was far-off thunder, but the sky was blue. He followed the river until he reached the canoe place a few miles away. He had come here once with Little Beaver. They had stopped to watch the men building canoes. Now it was deserted. Thomas picked his way around the half-finished canoes, feeling the emptiness of the place.

Thomas remembered watching the men take two long strips of cedar and tie them together at both ends with roots from a black spruce. Then they had forced the two cedar strips apart with planks and had driven stakes in the ground to outline the shape.

A second canoe was further along. The frame for this one had been carefully placed on top of a long piece of birch bark, with stones left on the crossbars to hold them down. The canoe had bark partially fitted around the sides. It was tied to stakes, making a clamp to hold it in place. The canoe makers had left their tools scattered about.

Thomas suddenly sniffed the air. He had come too far now to see the village, but he thought he smelled smoke. There was a gray haze in the air, and in the middle a thin plume of smoke.

It took him nearly an hour to get back. He saw

the devastated cornfield first. The valley seemed alive with soldiers. They were swarming over the village like locusts, destroying everything in sight. They were so intent on their destruction that he had not yet been noticed. He stepped over the burned stalks. He saw that the orchards had already been destroyed. The smaller trees had been cut down; the bigger ones girdled with an ax— they would be dead next spring.

Suddenly, the awful truth hit him. The people had managed to escape, but what of the days to come? Without food, how could they survive the winter?

Thomas had taken only a few paces from the fence when a shot rang out from a wooded area at the end of the devastated fields. The bullet passed so close to his head that he felt the wind at its passing. He dropped flat on the ground. The nearest cover was a hundred feet away, across the field. He would never make it.

"Sergeant Dixon, can you see him?" called a voice.

"He's in the grass there, Lieutenant," came the answer. "Soon as he raises his head, I'll get him."

Thomas suddenly realized that anyone seeing him would assume he was an Indian. "Hey," he yelled. "I'm an American."

There was silence for a moment and then the sergeant said, "Be careful, sir. It could be a trick."

"It's not a trick," Thomas yelled. "I'm Thomas Bowden. I was kidnapped by the Tories. I've been living here with the Mohawk, but I am an American."

"Well, I'll be," said the crusty voice of the sergeant. "Bowden, did you say? Where is your pa?"

"Last I heard, he was with General Washington, marching to New York," Thomas answered. "That was months ago."

"Well, I'll be," the sergeant said again. "I believe I know your pa. Better than that. I know where he is right this minute. Stand up, boy. If you have curly hair, you'll be safe enough."

Thomas felt his hair. It had grown long this past year, but the unruly curls remained. Slowly, he stood up.

Four soldiers appeared out of the woods. The one with the sergeant's stripes smiled. "Your pa talks about you all the time. He's pretty proud of you. Got a sister named Emma, too, if I remember, and a baby brother." He walked around Thomas. "I sure wouldn't have guessed you weren't an Indian." He touched Thomas's bow. "Can you shoot that thing?"

Thomas nodded. "Please, sir. You said you know about my father?"

The lieutenant stepped forward. "We've got a wagonload of wounded we're taking back to Fort Sullivan, just north of the Wyoming Valley. Your father is there. His enlistment is up, but he's been searching for you. It was like you dropped off the face of the earth."

Thomas looked back at the village. "Why did you do this?"

The lieutenant nodded grimly. "We're going to chase every one of those murdering savages out of this country. Our orders come straight from General Washington himself. We're to see to it that they have no reason to come back. I imagine that's good news to you."

Thomas did not answer. How could he make the

lieutenant understand? A few months ago he had felt the same way. Now, thinking of the happy times he'd spent here, the news made him feel only sadness.

The sergeant looked at Thomas. "Still, it's kind of a shame. It was a pretty little town."

"I wonder where the people went," Thomas said.

"We fired our cannons ahead," the sergeant said. "Gave them a chance to clear out. Most will head for Canada, I suppose. Too late to replant their crops."

Thomas just stared, scarcely believing he had slept through the cannon fire.

The wagon of wounded caught up and the lieutenant gave the order to move out. Thomas looked back at the village. Men were moving about with torches. Several cabins were already blazing. Suddenly, Thomas broke loose. "Wait!" he screamed.

Thomas sprinted the distance to his home of the last months. He ran inside and looked around, wondering what he should save. His claw necklace was there on his sleeping skin. He put it around his neck. The bearskin was heavy, but he rolled it up.

"You have to get out of here, boy," a soldier said, sticking his head in the door. Already flames were crackling, and the smoke made him choke. He went outside, not looking at the bench he had made for Laughs-at-Rain as a soldier chopped it with an ax and threw it in the flames.

Thomas fell in step beside the sergeant. He did not look back.

The sergeant patted him on the back. His eyes looked kind. "Less than a week, you'll be with your pa again. I imagine you'll have a lot to tell him."

Thomas nodded. He walked straight and tall beside the soldiers. He did have a lot to tell his father. He could not forget the terrible sight of the scalps being sold to the British. Still, in a war there were unforgivable things done on both sides. That was the trouble with war. The enemy became monsters and you never learned that they were people often very much like yourself. People who could be your friends, or even someone you loved.

There had to be a way for them to live together, respecting one another for their differences. He would tell other people, too. He closed his eyes and said a silent prayer that they would listen.

More about *Thomas in Danger*

Philadelphia was a modern bustling city in Thomas's time. It had been carefully planned with wide streets and parks. But little crooked alleys grew between the streets, and this is where many of the craftsmen lived and had their shops.

In the early days of the city the streets were muddy and filled with garbage. A law was passed in 1750 requiring homeowners to keep the streets clean in front of their houses. It was mostly ignored. Gradually the streets were paved, and at Benjamin Franklin's urging scavengers, or street cleaners, were hired.

Many children learned a trade by being apprenticed to a craftsman. They were taught such reading and writing as might be needed for the job. But the Quaker founders of Philadelphia started schools, many of them free. Most children, however, attended only a few years, except for those from wealthy families.

Most cities had poorhouses or poor farms for people who were homeless or unemployed. Residents worked for a meager existence. People who could not pay their debts were sent to prison until family or friends could pay the money they owed.

In the winter of 1777–1778, George Washington and his men suffered with cold and hunger at Valley Forge. But just a few miles away, the British soldiers passed a comfortable winter in the city. They stabled their horses at the market and used the state house and the Walnut Street prison to house prisoners of war. Many prisoners died from hunger and disease. The officers stayed in private homes, sometimes forcing the owners to live in the servants' quarters. Tories entertained the officers with dinners and parties, but when the British left the city many of the Tories fled with them.

The Liberty Bell, engraved with the words *Proclaim Liberty throughout all the land unto all the inhabitants thereof*, was first hung in the Pennsylvania state house in 1753. It was rung at the signing of the Declaration of Independence on July 4, 1776, as well as for other important events until 1846. A small crack had widened too much for the bell ever to be rung again. During the British occupation, it was hidden, along with the bell from Christ Church, because the colonists feared the bells would be melted down to make bullets. After the British left, the bells were quickly brought back.

There were about one hundred thousand Iroquois people living in the rich hunting and planting lands along the Saint Lawrence River and around the eastern Great Lakes when the European colonists first arrived. They were a fierce and proud people, really an alliance of five nations: the Mohawk, Oneida, Cayuga, Seneca, and Onondaga. Later they became the six nations when the Tuscarora joined with them.

The alliance put an end to the constant war among the five nations. It was such a strong form of government that some historians believe the founding fathers considered it when creating our own.

Contact with white settlers was devastating to the Iroquois. Thousands died from the white man's diseases of smallpox and measles. Hoping to stop the settlers from taking any more of their lands, they sided with the British in the Revolutionary War.

Iroquois was a derisive name given them by their bitter enemies, the Algonquin Indians. The Iroquois called themselves Haudenosaunee, meaning "people of the long house."

When the settlers first arrived, the Iroquois did live in longhouses built of wood and birch bark. Sometimes as many as twenty families lived together in one house. Each family had its own space and fire pit with only holes in the roof for ventilation. The houses were so smoky that many of the older people had severe breathing problems and even went blind from the irritation to their eyes.

Because the Iroquois often surrounded their villages with strong walls, the settlers would call them castles. By Thomas's time, however, many Iroquois lived in houses much like his own in frontier Pennsylvania, except that, instead of a chimney, there was a hole in the roof just like in the longhouses. Each town usually had at least one longhouse to be used for council meetings, in which Iroquois women enjoyed great respect.

Joseph Brant really did exist. His Mohawk name was Thayendanagea, meaning "strength." After his home was burned down by settlers, he and his warriors stayed close to the British Fort Niagara in Ontario. From there he and the Tory leader John Butler led the attacks on the frontier settlements. The settlers often called Joseph Brant "monster Brant," but the loss of lives was always much less when he was present at a battle.

George Washington did order his soldiers to destroy crops as a means of eliminating the Iroquois. The army would do so just before harvest, when it was too late to replant. The soldiers were amazed to find vast fields of corn, beans, and squash, and orchards of apples, peaches, and plums. At one town they destroyed twenty thousand bushels of corn. The following winter was one of the worst on record. Driven from their homes and broken in spirit, thousands of Iroquois died of hunger and disease. At the end of the war there were only about five thousand Iroquois left, mostly in Canada.